CLOUDY WITH A CHANCE OF GUNFIRE

Also by Lawrence W. Erickson

A Bullet For The Cartel
A Bullet For The Republic
A Bullet For Your Thoughts

CLOUDY
WITH A CHANCE OF
GUNFIRE

- Nate Harver Private Investigator Series -

LAWRENCE W. ERICKSON

LUMINARE PRESS
WWW.LUMINAREPRESS.COM

Cloudy With a Chance of Gunfire
Copyright © 2022 by Lawrence W. Erickson

All rights reserved. This book or any portion thereof may not be reproduced or used in any manner whatsoever without the express written permission of the publisher, except for the use of brief quotations in a book review.

Printed in the United States of America

Luminare Press
442 Charnelton St.
Eugene, OR 97401
www.luminarepress.com

LCCN: 2022905598
ISBN: 978-1-64388-956-6

This book is for Kate, always.

PROLOGUE

Dawn broke across the Oregon Cascade Range. Mt. Hood came into majestic relief above a Columbia Blacktail doe standing vigil at the edge of the tree line. Her two fawns nibbled blueberries from the bush they hid behind. She calmly, yet attentively, continually surveyed her surroundings. She sensed no threat from two men working near the base of the hill a hundred yards below. Even the ancient excavator was no concern. The breeze carried belching diesel fumes and noise away from her, toward the rickety farmhouse a half mile to the west. She and her young were safe.

The two men worked with little verbal communication. They'd performed this task before.

Once the trench was cut into the base of the hill, the operator shut off the engine and climbed from the cab. Tall and heavy, he was shirtless with large muscular arms and dressed in mud splattered bib overalls. Wiry blond hair stuck out of a ragged NRA cap. He casually studied the other man who was tightening a burlap tarp around an object resting on the small two-wheeled trailer behind the back hoe.

The second man, smaller in stature was hatless and balding. Dressed in Khakis and a green Polo shirt, he took two shovels from the bed of the trailer and walked to the side of the trench. He handed one to the driver. "Can't believe the backhoe's still running. We were kids when uncle John brought it home. You remember that day, Rowdy? My old man had a shit hemorrhage cause your dad paid a hundred and fifty dollars for it."

Rowdy drove his shovel into the pile of red dirt next to the trench. "They was always arguing, 'cept when they had a woman here. Pa said this thing paid for itself a hundred times." He motioned to the trailer. "Your pa put that together from parts he scrounged at the junkyard in Sandy. He was sure enough good with his hands, Bernie."

Bernie said, "They both were. Taught us a lot." He pointed the tip of his shovel to the burlap tarp. "Not that this skill is very marketable."

Rowdy laughed. "Marketable? That a word you learned in college and use on the news?"

"Nope. But the guy giving the stock market report uses it. Not much opportunity to discuss marketing on the weather report."

Rowdy nodded. "Okay, Mr. TV Weatherman. You see them clouds off behind you? Their tellin' me we're about to get our butts soaked if we don't get a move on."

Bernie turned and scanned the dark sky to the west. "You may be right, cousin. Let get this thing in the trench."

They walked to the trailer, each grabbing a handful of burlap.

Halfway back to the trench, Rowdy asked, "Wanta say a few words?"

Bernie almost lost his grip on the bundle. "You gotta be kidding! Where did that come from? You're not watching the 700 Club? I swear to God, if you start in on that stuff again…"

"Nah, Bernie. I just thought… You know."

"No. I don't know. You let this get personal and who knows where that'll lead. Just toss this thing in the goddamn trench."

The cousins swung and let go. With a thump, the burlap landed six feet below them and flopped open. A grey arm with a tattooed sleeve of roses wrapping from elbow to shoulder slipped onto the damp red earth.

The wind shifted to the east.

The doe and her fawns bolted from the blueberry bush. It was not safe. They smelled death and darted up the hill to shelter in the dense forest of fir trees.

CHAPTER 1

Friday, early September

Orlando was nervous, and that's unusual. There wasn't even a gun pointed at him. Come to think of it, he wouldn't be nervous at all if there was a gun pointed at him. That's when he gets calm – real calm.

With his back to me, he stared out our office window for the fifth time in the last ten minutes. Shoving his hands into the pockets of his cream-colored linen slacks, he grunted, "It's gonna rain. There's even talk of hail." Watching Orlando pout was a once in a lifetime experience.

"The weatherman said the rain wouldn't get north of Corvallis." I turned back to my laptop and opened Leo Freytag's latest email. Leo's the Manager of Fraudulent Claims for Lumberjack Mutual Insurance Company. Orlando and I do Leo's dirty work and make him look good to his superiors. He likes our work and compensates us more than decently.

"What's the weatherman know?" Orlando was not moving off his stance on doom and gloom. "I'll be bankrupt by Monday."

"Calm down. How much did you sink into the vineyard?"

"Too much."

"Come on, you won't be standing on a street corner, cup in hand."

He was still staring out the window. I started to tell him it was impossible to see Ribbon Ridge and the vineyard from there, then thought better of it. "You know what Donnie said about investing in vineyards?"

"Tell me. What did Donnie say?"

"That's the way you turn a large fortune into a small fortune."

He still had his back to me. "Then I guess I'm in luck. I only invested a small fortune."

"Why don't you give Amber Waves a call? Maybe Ellis knows about some African kingpin who needs toppling. You two can go over and rob their treasury. While you're at it, bring freedom to the downtrodden masses."

"Been there. Done that."

I nodded at the computer screen. "Yeah. I know."

Orlando turned around and asked, "You give any more thought to hiring someone to do the bookkeeping, answer phones when we're away, and generally keep the office going?"

I said, "I think we're fine the way we are."

Orlando leaned against the wall. "Ellis is handing over more of his responsibility to me. When he retires, I'll be swamped."

"Is Amber Waves giving you a raise?"

He nodded. "Of course. You think I stick my neck out for free?"

"Thought you signed up to be a mercenary for the camaraderie and butt slapping."

"That too. But the money helps. Find somebody, and I'll fork over seventy-five percent of the salary."

I wrote myself a note to call a temp agency. "I'll look into it."

I sat back in my chair contemplating the impact of Ellis, a senior executive in one of the world's largest private armies, retiring. "There are a few very dangerous folks around the globe who'll breathe a sigh of relief when Ellis steps off stage."

Orlando said, "I don't plan on giving them a chance to take that breath."

I had to agree. There was a ton of truth in that statement.

Orlando brightened up. "Come to think of it, I do need to give Ellis a call. I should buy him dinner. All he got from the FBI was a 'thank you' for helping out with that Spanish pervert last spring. And speaking of Spanish, there's a great new tapas place in Marina Del Ray I want to try. He'll like that. So will Torres. Maybe I'll get that Singapore Airlines flight attendant I met last week to go along." His mood was definitely improving.

I reached across the desk for a file on one of Leo's hard cases. Fire shot through the muscle in my stomach, and my hand began to shake.

Ever vigilant, Orlando caught it. "Still hurts, huh?"

"Only when I forget about it and do something stupid."

"A wound like that needs time to heal."

"Never been shot in the stomach before. Takes some getting used to."

Orlando reached for his cellphone. "I've stopped my fair share of bullets, never one to the gut." He looked back at me. "That crazy old woman is coming up for trial in a week or two. You'll be busy with that for a while."

I sat back in the chair. The pain was going away. "*Crazy* is the key word. That will be the defense's summation, and I tend to agree."

One of the senior residents in my condo association, a Ms. Merriman, had shot me while we were together in the building's elevator. When she was about to step off into the lobby, her Shih Tzu Harold made its usual lunge for my ankle and connected. I'd just bounced the little monster off the elevator wall when I looked up to see a tiny revolver in her hand. I remember a flash that coincided with a loud noise and then sliding down to the floor. My last recollection was of Harold standing on my chest licking the blood off my shirt.

Even a shooting can have a silver lining. The Portland Police, specifically Captain Art Mickelson, had tied the revolver to the murder of an FBI agent. The agent, unfortunately, had parked his souped-up Chevy El Camino in Ms. Merriman's parking slot a few weeks earlier. The police, the FBI – and yours truly – assumed the agent had been assassinated by a very nasty Mexican drug lord named Avonaco Jauregi, or to his friends *El Viho*. The mistake regarding who had shot the FBI agent led to a string of misconceptions, errors on the part of every law enforcement agency in the state, and a pile of dead bodies. Among the dead were a multitude who deserved it, and a few who didn't.

One of those who didn't deserve to die was my partner, mentor and father figure, Donnie Shepard. Donnie had also been Orlando's father in every sense of the word, except by blood. Years ago, Donnie pulled Orlando, then a tiny child, out of a container full of dead people being smuggled into the USA from Central America.

Sometime after that, I saved Donnie's life by shooting a crazed killer who'd put two rounds in his back. He liked the way I'd responded and brought me into his investigation agency.

Donnie raised Orlando and, to a large degree me, to be the men we are today.

I guess all that is another story.

The only concern on our immediate horizon was the upcoming grape harvest in the valley. Orlando had taken a large chunk of his semi-ill-gotten gains from Amber Waves, along with a big piece of his legally earned cash, and invested with a local vintner whose plan was to extend his acreage. A few of Orlando's buddies from the fringe world of mercenaries threw some of their stash into his investment. Knowing these guys on a personal basis, I seriously doubted the sanity of the vintner. Over the past several years, the vineyard rode the Oregon Pinot Noir wave. Seventy to one hundred dollars was a lot to pay for a bottle of wine, but there appeared to be a fair number of people around the world willing to do just that. Of course, it helped if there was a good vintage and right now that was the elephant in the room.

Orlando scooped up his cellphone and returned to the window to keep up the vigil.

I made one last swipe at my email before I called it a day and headed for the Noble Rot. A thirty-year-old, recently divorced, interior designer I met while in the hospital would be joining me for a marvelous view of the city, cocktails and small plates – followed by a hands-on appraisal of my condo. At our initial encounter in the fifth-floor hallway at Providence Hospital, we were both strolling along with IV drips and dressed to the nines in hospital johnnies – hers much more stylish than mine. I'd just had three bullets extracted. She was recovering from an appendectomy. Not exactly similar surgeries, but close enough for us to have something in common.

I scrolled down the mountain of emails from Best Buy, Macys, Land's End, and a few radical Political Action Committees that somehow had me on their mailing list. After deleting them, I hovered over the junk mail a tad too long and there it was – the last thing I wanted to see on a nice Friday afternoon. Buried there was a message from the dark side. Cliffy was on my trail.

CHAPTER 2

Friday evening

Cliffy Hasick is the bottom rung on Portland's criminal ladder. As far as I know, he may be the bottom rung for the whole of Oregon. Donnie once told me a few rivals for that honor reside along the coast in Lincoln City and farther south around Klamath Falls. I've not, as of yet, had the pleasure of crossing paths with these pillars of their communities. For the time being, Cliffy proudly wears that mantle within the unsavory element of our fair city.

Not long ago, Cliffy was instrumental in the recovery of some stolen goods. The tools and car parts had been pilfered from an auto repair shop in Cliffy's neighborhood. The garage owner was also a close friend of mine and a Marine Corps buddy to Donnie. Around the same time Cliffy was preforming this civic duty, he fell in love. The light of his life was Felicienne, a gorgeous young woman of French and Asian descent. Just to prove the universe is completely out of balance, she appeared to genuinely have similar feelings toward Cliffy. If I think about this subject too long, I'd end up in the nearest bar drinking myself into a stupor.

I scrolled the mouse back and forth over Cliffy's email – from delete to open.

Decisions, decisions.

Masochism won. I tapped open.

"Natekins, need to talk soon. Desperate. Please call ASAP. Clifford."

I felt the rest of the day starting to spin out of control. My hand, with a life all of its own, reached for the cellphone.

The phone rang at the other end. I could imagine what it sounded like in the bowels of The Sweet Mackerel, Cliffy's strip club and dive bar. I waited, expecting a barely legal teenage stripper to answer.

When the receiver was lifted at the other end no pulsating, eardrum shattering AC/DC chant greeted me. It was oddly silent.

"Sweet Mackerel, this is Barbie." God, she sounded like a fifth grader.

I wanted to scream, "Barbie, see that door with the shower curtain over it? Drop the phone, run out, and never come back." Instead, I asked, "Is Cliffy there?"

This seemed a very difficult question for her to grapple with. A few mumbles came across the line. Perhaps she was conferring with the other girls. The meek voice came back on. "Cliffy's not feeling so well right now. Maybe you better call back later."

"Tell him Nate is on the phone."

It sounded like she set the phone down.

A good minute passed.

Then, "Nate?"

"Cliffy, what's the problem?"

He groaned, "Oh, Nate." Followed by the sound of wet sobs. I think his phone hit the floor.

More silence.

"Cliffy?"

"She's gone, Nate. She's gone."

"Who's gone, Cliffy?"

"Felicienne. I can't find her. Something's really wrong. Oh, Nate. I need to see you."

My immediate reaction was that the beautiful Felicienne had finally come to her senses.

"Cliffy, I'm meeting someone this evening."

"Please, Nate. Just come out for a minute. Please. This is driving me crazy. Please."

Out-of-body, I watched myself make a major mistake. "Okay, Cliffy. But only for a minute."

"Thank you. Thank you. Nate?"

"What?"

"Hurry."

I hung up.

Orlando left his post by the window and walked over to his tea stash on the counter. "That Cliffy?"

"Excellent deduction."

"I went to private-eye school." He picked out a tea-leaf container that met his rigid standards.

"He needs to see me, right away."

"And, you're going? Right away?"

"Yep, looks that way."

"Thought you had a date with the interior designer tonight."

"I do. I've just got time to drive out to Cliffy's and get back to town."

His ponytail swayed as he shook his head. "You are a sick, sick man."

CHAPTER 3

Friday evening

The drive east on Sandy Boulevard is not one I frequently take. The airport is out that way, but it's much easier to hop on Interstate 84 than to fight the traffic and stop lights on Sandy. With all of Portland redecorating, it shouldn't have surprised me that gentrification was catching fire along the boulevard. At least two brand-spanking-new brew pubs were up and running since the last time I'd made the drive. Several upscale boutiques and restaurants held sway in neighborhoods I'd written off long ago.

I pulled over and swung into the gravel parking lot surrounding the Sweet Mackerel. My jaw dropped. An earthmover and a dump truck took up most of the west side of the lot. A new foundation was being poured where the east parking lot had once been. The shabby structure Cliffy called home was still standing but listing to the south. A strong breeze might provide the *coup de grace*.

I maneuvered the pickup around the earthmover and parked behind the Mackerel. A large wheeled trash dumpster, which had once been blue, greeted me. Now it was one of those colors you just can't quite put a name to.

I stepped around the dumpster, and there he was. The forty-foot square hunk of grass had managed to survive the thousands of drunks who pissed and upchucked on it. To call it a lawn would be unfair to the other lawns in the city. In the center of the freshly mowed meadow sat a bright yellow chaise lounge. On the vinyl slats with a tall glass in one hand and a red cowboy bandana in the other reclined Cliffy.

He raised the bandana to his bulbous nose and gave out a honk that might make migrating geese change course. His odd-colored, yet finely tailored suit was a rumpled mess. His Allen Edmonds oxfords were scuffed. With the absence of Felicienne, Cliffy was returning to his old self.

Without acknowledging my presence, Cliffy began looking around for something for me to sit on, gave up, and swung his legs off the lounge. He raised the bandana and pointed to the slats he'd just uncovered. I really wasn't comfortable sitting quite that close to him.

Crossing my arms, I walked up to him. "Okay, Cliffy. Get it out. I'm pressed for time."

He looked up with tears in his eyes. "Oh, for Christ's sake, Nate. Sit down." He patted the vinyl. "I'm not contagious."

Fully knowing that was a blatant untruth, I took the risk. My freshly pressed khakis plopped down on the slats and God knows what else.

"Believe it or not, I went to the police first." The bandana was covering his mouth. It was hard to make out his mumbling. "The cop on the desk – he laughed at me."

The thought – *I can understand that* – crossed my mind, but not my lips.

"Cliffy, you haven't done a lot to endear yourself with the Portland PD."

Nodding his head, he looked down at the grass. "I know."

I looked at my watch. I was not going to be late for this date. "How long has she been gone?"

"Three days this morning."

"Did she just disappear?"

This time he shook his head. "Not really. She went out looking for one of our girls. Well, actually two of them."

"Why was she looking for them?"

"Maxine, one of our more dependable dancers, took off without notice last week. She never showed up for the morning shift. I thought it was strange, but you know how these girls come and go. Felicienne was upset. She tends to bond with some of the girls, being a former adult entertainer herself."

I wanted to correct him with *stripper*. But again, held my tongue.

Cliffy set his glass on the grass and put his hands on his knees. He hitched up a deep breath, which seemed to stabilize him. "Then, Tuesday morning Rowena didn't show. If anything, Rowena is more dependable than Maxine."

"So where was Felicienne going to look for the girls?"

"Well, first she called the number we have for Rowena. Rowena's mother answered. The woman was quite beside herself. Rowena has a young daughter. I guess the mother is the sitter. Anyway, Rowena never came home Monday night. The mother said that never happens."

"What about the other girl? Did you try to reach her?"

"Felicienne did. No answer and no voice mail. She tossed her iPad in her purse and drove off. At the time I was arguing with the delivery man from Eugene. Frankly, didn't pay it much attention." The bandana went for his nose again as a fresh torrent of tears streamed out.

I asked, "Felicienne didn't give you any clue as to where she was going?"

"I heard her say something like 'Better not be that creep on TV.' At least that's what I think I heard."

I glanced at my watch. Shit. I had fifteen minutes to get back to town. "Listen, Cliffy. Email me whatever you can on the girls and Felicienne. Anything you can think of. Okay?"

Lifting the glass and taking a long swallow, he nodded again. "Okay."

I stood up and started towards my pickup. "I'll see what I can do, Cliffy."

He reached out, touching my sleeve. "Thanks, Nate. I knew you'd help."

Leaving him to his misery, I got in the pickup, started it and rolled through the gravel and dust toward Sandy. In the side mirror, I watched Cliffy swing his rumpled trouser legs up on the yellow slats. The bandana covered his face.

I looked left, right, left and pulled out into the traffic.

CHAPTER 4

A wet one at kick off.

The RIP CITY News Team was wound tighter than a tennis racquet. Right after the six o'clock program, the newly installed LED lighting was switched on. The ten o'clock news was about to start, and every anchor's concern was more on their makeup than the prompter in front of them. Every anchor but Bernie. Bernie's attention wasn't on his makeup, or the weather chart behind him, nor the storm stalled off Astoria.

Bernie's mind was elsewhere.

He knew finding a woman to bring to the farmhouse wasn't necessarily going to be a problem. However, finding one to take to the National Meteorologist Awards Banquet – well, that was another story. Geez, every time he worked up the nerve to talk to some babe in a bar, she'd turn out to be a hooker. Worse yet, the ones with any interest in talking to him, and not looking to turn a trick, sure as hell weren't "10s".

The other night, after striking out in the Bellweather Lounge, he approached Chet, the anchor on the Sports Desk, for advice. "You always pickup tail here. What am I doing wrong?"

Chet, draining the last of his third double scotch, slurred, "Ah, screw it. Just pick an ugly one and put a bag over her head!" Then, Chet laughed his loud unbearable laugh.

Why didn't everybody at the station hate that laugh? Was he the only one? Charlene "With-The-Big-Tits" who filled in for Bernie on the weather slot every weekend, thought Chet was hot stuff. Chet had to be banging her. How could she stand that laugh?

Bernie allowed himself a quick fantasy involving Charlene down in the basement of his cousin's farmhouse. Yes sir! Then, we'd see who was hot stuff. His mind wandered a bit too long on that concept. Aw, Shit – he felt himself becoming aroused. His mind short-circuited to the new lights. Did they really pick up everything?

He'd be on in 10, 9, 8… seconds. The little blue light on the camera pointing at him turned red just as he heard Chet let out his goddamn laugh and bellowed, "Hey Bernie, are the Ducks gonna be playing in a foot of water tomorrow, or what?"

He was as hard as the marble columns in the studio lobby. Fuck! He lowered his hands, crossing them in front of himself while making a really uncomfortable turn to the right.

Bernie made one of his usual lame responses. "Ha ha, Chet. Looks like those web feet on the Ducks will come in handy this weekend." He felt his face getting hot. Shit! The camera would pick that up too.

From the corner of his eye, he saw Chet nudge Harlan, the anchorman. Both began giggling. Chet was rolling his eyes. Now Missy, the co-anchor with the creamy ebony skin and sexy eyes, was in on the joke. She put her hand over her mouth. Her big brown eyes were about to pop out of her fucking head. Fuck her, maybe she'd like a look at the basement.

Bernie raised his right hand and pointed to the imaginary map over his shoulder. Now, the cameraman was laughing. A snapshot of this guy's wife bending over the buffet table at the Christmas party flashed through Bernie's head. She's next.

Bernie grimaced at the camera. "That's right folks. The rain hanging over the coast all week will make its way to Eugene overnight. The Ducks and the Wildcats are in for a wet one at kick off!"

CHAPTER 5

Friday evening

It was five minutes past seven o'clock when I stepped onto the elevator that would carry me up four floors to the restaurant. I figured if I were in France, I'd be early. Orlando once told me if invited to a social occasion it's polite to be a few minutes late, but not polite to be a few minutes early. He had, unfortunately, chosen to provide that advice within earshot of Donnie. If I remember correctly, Donnie's comment was something along the lines of, "What are you? Fucking Emily Post?" With that, he grabbed his cowboy hat while storming out of the office shaking his head. His parting comment, "Where did I go fucking wrong?"

Orlando must've been right. My date, Abby, waved from the bar looking extremely happy to see me. I hoped my smile told her the feeling was mutual.

As she walked to me, every guy at the bar followed her with their eyes. Can't say I blamed them. Her long blond hair was accented by evening sunlight streaming through the west windows. Her grayish tan business suit was tastefully suggestive. Truthfully, I can't say I'd go through it all again to meet her. Not sure I could handle another bullet in the stomach. But it did look like we had a pleasant evening in front of us.

"Here's the man I've been waiting for."

She took my hand and gave me a kiss on the cheek that lingered a tad longer than a friendly peck. I told the maître d' we had a reservation. He checked the computer, gave me a nod, picked up two menus, and led us to out onto the rooftop dining area.

We walked around a large table of eight who appeared to be in the middle of their meal. I heard a smattering of Russian. All the men looked like the guys you see on the WWE TV channel. Mixed in with the Russian, I picked out "Harver". One who looked like Randy "Macho Man" Savage locked eyes with me. There was a big toothy smile on his face that didn't quite make it up to his eyes. He had a tight grip on a woman who looked like she ordered her outfit through Hustler magazine. His right hand was cupping her breast. His free hand came up like a pistol and pointed at me. The guy to Randy's left bore a strong resemblance to Ric Flair. Randy said something to Ric and laughed. Then everybody at the table looked at me.

The maître d' guided us to our table. We ended up across the room from the Russians. Once seated, I looked back at them. Something else must have grabbed their attention. Nobody was looking our way.

"Are we going to compare scars tonight?" Abby waved her hand at me. "Just trying to regain your attention."

I turned to her, more than a little embarrassed. "Sorry."

She grinned at me. "I hope you find me more attractive than that table of hairy bears."

I reached over for her hand. "Trust me, I do." I gave it a squeeze. "Thought I recognized somebody there. Not very polite of me."

"Buy me a drink. See if I can forgive you."

She ordered cocktails for both of us which turned out to be excellent. I'm not sure I could have pronounced them correctly anyway. The small plates we shared were as good as the cocktails. The bottle of Southern Oregon Tempranillo we split was right on the money. Who can ask for a better start to the evening? However, having said that, the body slammers four tables over still bugged me.

We capped it all off with a crème brûlée that has more than likely sent a multitude of diners to the emergency room for a heart stent. The waiter brought Abby an espresso with a Moscato grappa. I had an espresso but passed on the grappa, knowing I'd eventually need to get behind the wheel.

From the roof, the view of the city was magnificent. Night had fallen by the time we got up to leave. Across the Willamette River the tall buildings were brightly lit – Portland magic. I stepped around the table to help Abby up and heard my name again. This time louder and slurred. I looked over at Ric. He was pointing at me. The grip on his girl was as obnoxious as Randy's. The women looked confused. The other three men looked ugly. Drunk and ugly.

Abby gripped my hand. "Are they pointing this way?"

"I think they're mistaking us for someone else."

She turned to me. "Us? I'm pretty sure you're the one they're interested in."

We made our way to the elevator. Behind us I picked out three words mixed in with the drunken laughter – Harver, Cliffy, and *shasa*.

Two names I didn't appreciate being in the same sentence.

The last word had me stumped, "*shasa*".

Protector?

CHAPTER 6

Saturday morning

I woke up alone in my own bed. Not exactly the master plan I'd concocted the day before.

Abby and I'd been walking hand in hand down Burnside from the restaurant when she abruptly turned into the dark foyer of a closed coffee shop. Naturally, I followed her in. Before I could initiate any of my world-famous romantic moves, I felt her body press firmly against me. Her mouth was on mine and it felt really, really good. She tasted every bit as wonderful as I'd imagined she would – actually much better. At the same instant I realized our PDA was about to turn into something illegal, her cell broke into "Girls Just Want to Have Fun." Breathing hard, she stepped back.

She rummaged in her purse muttering, "Shit. Shit. Shit."

She found the phone and held it to her ear. "Deb, you could not have called at a worse time." She caught her breath. I hadn't caught mine yet. Her other hand pulled me close, and I buried my face in her neck. I heard her say, "This better be important."

I maneuvered us up against the wall of the dark enclave.

Then she said, "Yes. Yes. Yes. Well, seems I don't have much choice. You tell him."

She put the phone to my ear. Deb's voice was all giggles. "Hi. Guess I'm interrupting something?"

My voice was hoarse. "Lady, you have no idea."

Abby pressed against me. I made a slight gasp which prompted another giggle on the other end of the phone. I got myself half-way composed. "Well, Deb. I'd like to say it's a pleasure meeting you this way."

"I hate to do this to you two, but I need the gorgeous girl you seem to be entwined with."

"Entwined isn't exactly the descriptor, but it's definitely the direction we were heading."

"Sorry, handsome. And – from what I hear – you are. I just closed a three-million-dollar deal to revamp the skyboxes at Safeway Field. I'm walking back to our office with the owners. Wish all I needed was her brains, but the rest of her comes with them. Let's say I owe you one."

I handed the phone back.

We stepped out of the shadows and walked to the curb. Deb had called an Uber for Abby. It arrived much too quickly.

Abby gave me one last kiss and slipped into the back seat. I watched the tail lights until the car turned south on 11th.

After several deep breaths, I walked down the hill and got in my pickup. I put the key in the ignition. I could still feel her hand in mine.

Now, THE SUN WAS SHINING THROUGH THE PATIO DOOR. I got up and put together some Bob's Red Mill Blueberry Granola and yogurt. I sliced dates and threw them in. Two hard boiled eggs were left from the day before. I poured a tall glass of orange juice and sat down at the table by the windows. The view south went on forever. Part of my plan had been for Abby to enjoy the view with me. I glanced at a picture on the window ledge. It was a shot taken on Mount Hood at Timberline Lodge. My godson Spidey was in my arms, waving at Art, who had snapped the picture. We were there to get Spidey on skis for the first time. He was a natural, as was his adopted mother, Margaret. Art and I'd spent most of the time on our butts, but the kid was skiing around us like he had been doing it his whole life, all five years of it.

I let my mind wander to another plan I'd flirted with a year ago. I thought that, just maybe, I would adopt Spidey, Molly would come back, and we would live happily ever after. Things didn't work out that way. But now, I was Uncle Nate and loved the role I played in his life. Speaking of play, Spidey and I had a playdate that afternoon at Playdate PDX children's gym on NW 17th. He was crazy about the mazes, slides, and climbing frames. His favorite thing was throwing foam balls at the other kids. Margaret had not exactly bought into that yet, but Margaret wasn't going to be with us this afternoon.

Art and Margaret both work for the Portland Police Department. Art is the head of the Homicide Division. Margaret is the Chief Forensics Officer. Needless to say, their paths often cross. Sometimes their paths cross with mine and Orlando's. Art and I have been through some rough times. We faced issues folks in the city thought would never be reconciled. We've managed to weather the storms. Now things are good between us, largely on account of Spidey. I plan to keep things good. I learned my lesson from the irresponsible handling of my relationship with Molly. She was gone from me for good. I was never going to let that happen with Spidey, Margaret, and Art.

CHAPTER 7

How about you look next time.

"She's got a dick!" Bernie dropped the pruning shears he'd used to cut through the expensive lingerie.

Rowdy's head swiveled up. He dropped the roll of duct tape. "What the fuck!"

"How did this happen? Are you fucking blind?"

Rowdy didn't have an answer.

"Pick up the tape and get this guy tied down. If he wakes up, we got a problem."

The tape rolled across the floor. Rowdy took off after it.

Three minutes later they had the body taped firmly to the metal table.

Rowdy looked at the naked boy. "Jesus, Bernie, she was givin' me a knob job in the van. I swear, I thought it was a woman." Rowdy also thought it was the best knob job he'd ever paid for, and he'd paid for a lot of them.

Bernie picked up a tube of KY jelly and hurled it at his cousin. "Well, I'm not getting my rocks off over some guy. What, you think I'm a sicko or something? Not only do we NOT HAVE a chick tonight, now we got to figure out what to do with this trans motherfucker."

Rowdy, looking for a way out of the mess, said, "Guess we can kill him."

"Kill him? Of course, we're gonna kill him! What the

fuck else are we going to do?" Bernie wasn't just hot now, he was burning. "Where's your dad's gun? Where's Uncle John's pistol?"

"It's upstairs in the hallway closet. Why do we have to shoot him? Can't we just finish him the way we do the girls?"

"Are you a fucking homo? Go get the goddamn gun!"

Rowdy took the stairs three at a time. Bernie could hear Rowdy's size 16 rubber boots plodding the hallway upstairs. Bernie only wished Rowdy's brain was half as big as his feet. Jeez, how did he team up with this idiot in the first place?

How?

Well, the answer to that was obvious. They had been doing this forever, ever since they were little kids. They started with insects, worked their way up to snakes, and then small farm animals. The big "Ah Ha!" had been the hog. They'd been fourteen when they did the hog. That got them into an acre of shit with their dads. Their dads were brothers. Bernie thought back to the ass chewing he and Rowdy had been on the receiving end of. Looking back on it, it could have been a lot worse. In fact, now as he remembered it, he was sure his dad and his uncle thought it was pretty damn funny. Maybe these two apples hadn't fallen too far from those two trees. Bernie preferred not to think about his dad and Uncle John doing this kind of stuff.

Not long after the hog, they'd found a young girl, one of the homeless who wandered onto the farm once in a while. They'd made a real mess of her, but Bernie always said, "You got to start somewhere."

Where in the hell was Rowdy? Bernie bounded up the stairs and yelled down the hall. "Get your goddamn ass in gear. This son of a bitch is gonna wake up any second." Bernie barely had the words out of his mouth when he heard a moan, *followed by something falling in the basement.* "Jesus." *He walked across the hallway into the parlor. On the sofa was one of Grannie's old embroidered pillows. He grabbed it.*

Racing back down the stairs, pillow in hand, Bernie heard Rowdy's rubber boots hit the stairs behind him. The boy on the table raised his head, straining at the duct tape. The kid's eyes were the size of saucers. Bernie reached over and jerked the pistol out of his cousin's fat hand. He slapped the pillow down on the kid's face, pushing the head back on the table. His other hand pressed the barrel into Grannie's pillow.

Rowdy screamed, "Not the Peanut Gallery pillow!" *and leaped on Bernie's back.*

Too late.

Bernie squeezed the trigger. The gunshot hammered their ear drums. The smell of cordite filled their nostrils. The body on the table emptied its bowels.

Rowdy's weight pushed Bernie forward. They fell across the body.

"Oh no, Bernie! Grannie's pillow!" *Rowdy watched as the smoldering pillow slid off the boy's face. It flipped over on the way to the floor. Buffalo Bob's face was covered with gore. The top half of Clarabell was burning. Flub-a-Dub wasn't looking very good either.*

Rowdy slid off the table. He moved on hands and knees across the cool concrete floor. He reached out for the pillow, which was now officially on fire, and slapped at the flames. "Ah, Bernie, you didn't have to do this. Not Grannie's Peanut Gallery pillow. It was her favorite."

Bernie didn't realize it, but he'd raised the pistol. The end of the barrel was about two inches from the back of Rowdy's skull. Bernie's finger tightened on the trigger. A sob came out of his cousin. Bernie's hand relaxed. He looked down, com-

prehending how close he'd just come to providing a solution for a whole bunch of his own troubles.

Nope. No matter how bad things were now, they could be a hell of a lot worse. Bernie set the pistol on the end of the table.

Something rank overwhelmed the smell of cordite.

"Fuck." He gave Rowdy a noogie on the back of his head. "Get up. We gotta clean up this mess."

Two hours later, the basement was pretty much shipshape. The stink was gone and Bernie figured it could pass a visual inspection. He knew if a half-way competent policeman ever did a DNA swipe, he and Rowdy would be up shit creek. But the chance of that happening was slim to none.

Bernie climbed the stairs slowly this time. He was worn out.

Rowdy sat cross-legged in a chair at the Formica kitchen table, a half empty bottle of cream soda in his hand. Bernie walked over to the old Kenmore refrigerator and took out a Bud Light Lime. Bernie pulled a chair from the table and sat down. His cousin's eyes were on the bottle of cream soda.

"Sorry, Bernie."

Bernie looked at his cousin. "It's okay. Everybody fucks up once in a while."

"Guess I fucked up pretty bad, huh?"

"Yeah. Guess you did."

Rowdy took a swig of the cream ale. "We don't have a girl tonight."

Bernie slugged down half of the Bud Light Lime. "Well, there's always next time." He rubbed his hand on the cool bottle. "Oh, and next time? How about you look next time."

CHAPTER 8

Saturday afternoon

We were at PlayDate PDX. Or, for those residing outside metropolitan Portland, boot camp for preschoolers. Spidey was soaked with sweat. I wiped his face and rubbed his hair. His T-shirt was sopping wet.

As we left the house, Margaret had handed me a beach towel and a fresh T-shirt. Her parting words were, "You're going to need these." I'd tossed them into the front seat of the pickup.

From under the towel, he stuck out his right hand with the fingers spread apart. "Five more, Uncle Nate. Five more. Please, Uncle Nate."

"Okay, buddy. Five more minutes."

He bolted back to the giant play pen. We were now on our third set of *five more*. I picked a slice of carrot from the veggie pack we were sharing and dipped it in ranch dressing.

A chair scraped the floor next to me. "You eat like girl." When I turned to the voice, there was Ric Flair running a hand through his golden locks and giving me a Russian shit-eating grin. Don't ask me to explain how a Russian shit-eating grin differs from any other shit-eating grin. It just does.

"Maybe you a bunny rabbit." Ric seemed easily amused by his own jokes. This one really made him roll. When he caught his breath, he said, "I have kid too. See. One in red shirt." He pointed into the pen at a large boy who had a smaller boy pinned to the mat, pounding on his head.

Ric stood up. "Cheslav, stop hitting boy, or I whip your butt." That got another laugh out of Ric. "Kid think he tough guy." Ric shrugged. "Maybe he is."

Ric sat back down resuming our conversation, one-sided as it was, "Your kid. He a tough guy?"

I thought about that. "He can hold his own."

If Spidey had inherited his biological mother's genes, he could probably whip everybody's ass in the building, including Ric's and mine. Brigidia Fernandez had been a top-ranking lieutenant in one of Mexico's most vicious drug cartels. She had not gained that rank based on good manners.

Ric laughed again. This was getting a bit monotonous. "You must be tough guy too. Cliffy hire you. No?"

I dipped another carrot. "Don't know what you're talking about." I offered the carrot to Ric.

He looked at it like I'd just stuck my butt in his face.

"Don't like carrots? Okay, more for me." I popped it into my mouth.

He recovered quickly. "I hear you Cliffy's hero. You going to find his woman for him? Cliffy not man enough to find woman. Not man enough to keep woman if he find her." No laughter this time.

I reached for a slice of yellow zucchini. "What's your business with Cliffy? And by the way, what's your business with me?"

"Cliffy is Karolek's business partner."

"Can't say I know the man."

"Karolek new in town. Me too."

"Just what the city needs, more Russian gangsters", I said and took a dainty nibble off the end of the zucchini slice. I thought this might get Ric's distain, but it didn't seem to bother him.

"No. You full of propaganda bullshit. Not gangsters. Businessmen."

"So, pardon me, but I still don't see why we're having this conversation." I looked at my watch. Spidey's *five more* were just about up. Thanks to my new friend, there wasn't going to be another five.

I stood, caught Spidey's eye, and waved him in. Surprisingly, I didn't get pushback. He came bounding.

"We find Cliffy's woman. Cliffy not need your help."

I grabbed the towel and scooped up Spidey when he leaped onto the chair. "Time to go, big guy."

"Twist, Nate." Spidey pleaded. "Stop at Twist, Nate."

"Can do, my man." I picked up Spidey's shoes, bright orange to match his pants.

He started humming the theme to SpongeBob Square Pants. We turned toward the door.

Ric reached out and put his hand on my arm. If Spidey hadn't been in the other one, I would have hit him. "You understand? Cliffy our problem."

I looked at his hand. "No Ric, I don't understand."

He released his grip. "Why you call me Ric? My name Tusya. You remember that. Okay? Tusya."

"Sorry, you'll always be Ric to me."

Spidey and I walked out and got in the truck. Twist was six blocks west. He'd have to eat his yogurt alone. I wasn't hungry.

CHAPTER 9

Saturday evening.

Art held his arms out and Spidey jumped into them. "You're welcome to stay for burgers, Nate."

Spidey hugged his dad.

"Tired of me, huh?" I tickled Spidey's tummy where the Blazers T-shirt rode up.

He smiled into Art's eyes. "Nate took me to Twist!"

Art put a finger to his lips. "Cripes, don't tell Margaret."

Spidey did the same.

"I'd like to. A burger sounds tempting. But I need to make a stop across town."

"How is your new social acquaintance working out? Abby?"

"Abby's just fine. If I could get her away from her job once in a while, I just might find out how fine." I gave Spidey a pat on the back and handed Art the soaked T-shirt and towel.

Spidey threw me a high five as I stepped down from Art's front porch.

I gave him one back. "Say bye-bye to your mom."

Art and Spidey waved as I backed out of the driveway.

All was right with the world.

Sometimes I just can't help myself. When things are going well, I usually find a way to derail them. I drove out Sandy Boulevard to the Sweet Mackerel.

The backhoe and the earthmover had traded places. There appeared to have been some progress on the construction next to Cliffy's lean-to.

Instead of opening a door, I swept a shower curtain aside. The term *class joint* is not in Cliffy's vocabulary. Stepping in was a bit surreal. A meeting was in progress. A large piece of plywood had been set up on two sawhorses at the center of Cliffy's lounge area. Three guys in work clothes and hard hats, Cliffy, one of his strippers, and Randy Savage were looking at a construction drawing. I walked up to the group. The drawing was a floor plan of a multiroom structure. In the lower right corner was a title block. Inside it were the words *Sweet Mackerel Renovation Phase One*.

Randy Savage pointed to a large room on the floor plan. "Needs more doors."

One of the hard hats said, "If you want changes, you better make them now. We've been over this a dozen times. Once we pour the concrete, you're gonna be out of change orders. "Capeesh?"

"Yeah. Capeesh." Randy picked up a pencil and started making marks on the drawing. "Here and here. See?"

The hard hat began rolling up the drawing. "Okay, but after today no more changes. Got it?"

Randy nodded to Cliffy. "No more changes." Cliffy nodded back.

The hard hat looked at me. "You got something to add?"

Randy gave me a dismissive wave. "He not included." Then he turned to Cliffy and pointed to me. "What the fuck this guy doing here?"

Cliffy meekly replied, "Mr. Harver and I have business to discuss."

"You got business to discuss, you discuss with Karolek." He glared at me.

I smiled at him. "I recently had a conversation along these lines with your pal, Ric Flare. Guess he hasn't had a chance to update you."

Randy, AKA Karolek, or whatever his name was, gave me a confused stare. "Don't know any Ric." He turned to the bar, where another member of the WWE was pouring himself a tall drink from Cliffy's collection of cheap liquor, and asked, "You know who this fuck is talking about?" The guy at the bar gave him a shrug and downed two fingers of something clear.

I motioned to Cliffy. "Tell this guy and his friend not to let the door hit them in the ass."

Karolek / Randy pointed to the entrance. "No door. Bathtub curtain." He seemed pleased with this observation.

I had to smile. "Right you are."

Cliffy headed for the rear exit, which miraculously had a real door. "Come out back, Nate."

I followed him.

The Neanderthal walked over to the old juke box and started pushing buttons. He yelled to my back, "Don't let door hit your skinny ass." Both Russians found this hilarious.

As I stepped outside, I heard the first bars of "Dark Star" from Jerry Garcia's guitar. "Cliffy, are there Deadheads in Russia?"

He stopped in the middle of his *lawn*. One of the workmen fired up the backhoe. "Shit, you can't hear yourself think around here." He stepped around the yellow chaise lounge and walked across the gravel towards Sandy Boulevard. I stayed hot on his trail.

We eventually reached a patch of flat concrete resembling a sidewalk. Cliffy took off down it. I wondered if we were going to walk to the airport.

Two blocks further we reached a bus stop with a metal bench. Cliffy plopped down on the bench with his arms crossed. "I may have erred."

That goes without saying, I thought. Instead, I said, "And, in what way did you err?"

"Letting Felicienne talk me into doing business with Karolek." He scratched his arm pit. The old Cliffy was almost back. "It sure seemed like a good idea at the time. She'd generated spreadsheets and everything. We'd be rolling in the money."

Thinking about Cliffy being involved in a real business deal, legit or otherwise, was putting a strain on me. "When did she come up with this idea?"

"Oh, she saw the potential the club has. She did her homework, ran the numbers, developed a business plan, did a cash flow analysis, checked the competition. She did it all."

A city bus pulled up and the door came open. The driver looked at us. Cliffy waved him away. The driver gave us the finger as he closed the doors. Maybe he and Cliffy had a history.

"So, you want out of this deal with the Russians?"

"No." He gave the other armpit a healthy scratch. "Felicienne has a good plan. She was project managing the whole renovation. It's just so damn hard without her." Cliffy now had on his dejected face. It wasn't any prettier than any of his other faces.

He looked up at me. "I want you to find Felicienne. Karolek thinks she just ran off with some guy. Felicienne would never do that. We had a commitment with each other. We're soulmates."

Cliffy with a soul, let alone a mate? What is the world coming to?

"Well, I told you I'd see what I can come up with. Not much to go on." I thought back to our conversation on Cliffy's yellow chaise lounge. "You said something about a creep from the TV station?"

Cliffy, with his elbows on his knees, bent forward and scratched his head with both hands. I guess he'd run out of arm pits. "There's this guy on the local news station who comes in a lot. The girls don't like him. His weirdo buddy comes in with him, a relative, I think? They drop a fair chunk of money on the girls. Good customers."

"But, Felicienne doesn't like him, or them?"

"Says they give her the creeps. Jesus, ninety percent of the guys that walk in the place would give you the creeps. Just part of doing business." That was quite an observation coming from Cliffy.

He leaned back on the bench and crossed his arms and ankles. His chin dropped to his chest. I stood there a few more minutes watching a deep blue funk descend over him. Another bus pulled up, but the driver didn't open the door. He looked at us through the long dirty vertical window and then drove off. I figured the driver had the right idea. I began walking the two blocks back to the Sweet Mackerel and my pickup. Half way back, I turned and looked at Cliffy. He hadn't budged. It appeared he wasn't aware I'd left.

CHAPTER 10

Monday morning

Art was pissed. "When did you start hanging out with human traffickers? Margaret is fit to be tied. I assume that gives you an indication of the current mood I'm in?"

I hadn't even had my first cup of coffee, and Art was all over me.

I said, "What are you talking about?"

"What am I busting your balls over? I'll tell you what I'm busting your balls over. Karolek. Him and his team of Muscovite scumbags. Oh, and speaking of scumbags, your pal Hasick is up to his degenerate eyeballs in whatever these Russians have going on."

Christ on a crutch. I sunk down in the chair; my hand gripping the cellphone. "Well, Art – thanks for the rosy update – first thing on a Monday morning."

"You can thank me by staying the hell away from that shithole strip bar. What were you doing there anyway? Never mind. I don't want to know the answer to that."

"Cliffy's girlfriend disappeared. He asked me to look for her." I glanced at my cowboy boots. They needed a buffing.

"You mean she came to her senses. Cliffy with a girlfriend, sounds unnatural. If she's missing, why didn't he come to the police? File a missing person's report?"

"He did. Your folks laughed at him. Told him to get lost."

Art was quiet for a few seconds. "Yeah, I can imagine the conversation. Cliffy hasn't done much to endear himself to the Portland PD, or anybody else come to think of it."

"So, who turned me in for collaborating with the bad guys? I bet it was an underage stripper you guys planted in the Sweet Mackerel." I stood and went over to the coffee pot.

"There's been a task force on Karolek for months. Human Trafficking and Youth Services Divisions. Thank God, not Homicide. It's all tied in with the Polaris Project and YES, the local Youth Ending Slavery group."

"Tell Margaret I'll steer clear of the Russians. I'm not interested in getting involved in that mess. Someone else can save the world."

"You can tell her yourself tomorrow when you pick up Spidey. I'm already on her shit list just from being in the room when she got the call on you from Bonnie Pardew over in Sex Crimes."

"I dated Bonnie for a while."

"A short while, I assume?"

"Short and not so sweet. No doubt it made Bonnie's day seeing my name pop up on a task force report."

"You and women. You ever gonna fix that problem?"

"That's just one of many I don't seem to have a solution for."

"Roger that."

Art broke the connection. He must have had better things to do than talk to a know associate of the Russian mob.

Fucking Cliffy. Getting involved with his troubles just proves the path to hell is paved with good intentions.

I sipped my coffee and wondered if the day could get any worse.

It did.

CHAPTER 11

Monday afternoon

The balance of the morning was spent with Leo. He was bent out of shape over a fifty-year-old woman from Hillsdale. She'd been awarded mucho bucks after receiving burns to her hands and legs in a Beaverton Korean Barbeque kitchen. Now, it was rumored she was driving a bus for an assisted living complex in Forest Grove. I'd made a few trips to the complex but hadn't turned up anything to give grounds to the rumor.

Just before I headed for a late food carte lunch, Leo's parting words to me were, "I got this from one of my more dependable snitches. Go back out there, Nate baby, and get the goods on this gal."

I hung up and looked at my watch. It was a quarter to two. By now, all of the ginger carrot soup in Spade's Hearty Soup cart would be gone. It probably wasn't worth the eight blocks walk up to Alder and 11th Avenue, but I needed some air. Art's ass-chewing was still ringing in my ears. I should have known better. Cliffy is a magnet for this kind of crap.

Sure enough, the ginger carrot soup was crossed off the menu at Spade's. Even the tomato with basil bisque was sold out. What's a food cart gourmet to do at a time like that? In the next stall was Milo's Slovenian Schnitzel cart. I looked in the greasy window. Old Milo had fallen asleep with his head against the window. Lack of customers can do that to a guy like Milo. I never figured out how he'd managed to stay in business. Another Portland culinary mystery.

My eyes traveled down the block past two burrito carts, the fish and chips shop, the Carolina Pulled Pork Kitchen, and came to a halt on the Vietnamese banh-mi sandwich cart. Two or three shrimp bahn-mi sliders washed down with a café sau da ice coffee would hit the spot.

With no need to wake him, I'd started walking softly past Milo when a vice clamped onto my right bicep.

"Harver, you got minute?"

Someone had taken a bath in a bottle of Brut. The smell was over whelming. Feeling the reassuring weight of the .38 Police Special tucked into the small of my back, I turned towards the odor.

Karolek was at the far end of the arm. The hand on the near end still held my jacket in a firm grip. The smile on his broad flat face wasn't working. I was thinking about advising him to look into a Dale Carnegie course at Portland State University, but wasn't sure they offered it.

Karolek wasn't the source of the smell. It was reeking off the giant in the dark leather trench coat standing next to him. The guy had to be over seven feet tall with more hair than Orlando. A few years back, Donnie scored front row tickets to a Blazers game. Our eyes glazed over in misery as seven-foot-six Yao Ming and the Houston Rockets gave it to Portland in the chops. Yao had been only a few feet from us for a good portion of the game. This guy, I was now looking in the crotch, could tell you if Yao had a bald spot.

The giant leaned against the Schnitzel cart, giving it a good jolt. Milo jerked awake. He slid the window open, sticking his fist out and waving it at the giant. "Hey, get your fat ass off my cart."

The giant turned to Milo, giving him a smile full of crooked brown teeth. "*Otvyazhis'. Eblan.*"

Milo's bald head went beet red. "*Ee-dee nah hooy!*"

The giant laughed, raising two fingers in the V sign. "*Otebis.*"

Milo slammed the window shut. I wasn't one hundred percent sure, but I think they'd told each other to fuck off.

Turning their attention back to me, the giant took my left arm and we marched off down the street.

"Need some privacy for conversation." Karolek and his friend made an abrupt right turn as the side door on a big white Mercedes van slid open.

The next thing I knew, I was lifted off my feet and tossed into a comfortable leather seat inside the van. The door slid back shut. Karolek and the giant settled into similar seats on both sides of me. In retrospect, I can't say the giant ever settled. He looked comfortably cramped. From the driver's seat Ric gave me a wave. "Hi, smart ass private eye."

"Ric, nice to see you."

Karolek gave me a confused stare. "Who the fuck is Ric? That is Tusya."

Tusya shook his head and turned around. "Dumb shit make same mistake with me. Call me Ric, all the time." He stuck his face in a porno magazine he'd been reading and appeared to be enthralled with the contents.

I made myself cozy. "Sorry, old habits are hard to break." I was getting the feeling this little get-together might last a while.

The giant laughed and uttered his first words in my direction. "How about we break your habit, dumb shit?"

Karolek patted me on the arm. "Now, now, you guys, be nice to mister private eye. Maybe he not so dumb after all." That got a grunt out of Ric. The giant belched and laughed again.

"Okay, enough of humor, Romeo. You too, Tusya. No more comment." Karolek was getting down to business.

Romeo? The other two shut up, which I took as a good sign.

"Maybe I jump gun with you at Sweet Mackerel." Karolek picked up a bottle that looked like crystal from a side bar and poured something clear into two glasses.

Ric looked up from the porn magazine.

Karolek barked at him. "None for you, asshole. You got to drive. Put your face back in pussy magazine. Maybe you see sister in there." Romeo roared with laughter and kicked the door of the van. The clear liquor splashed out of the glass and onto Karolek's designer jeans. "Stupid fucking imbecile." He glared at Romeo. "No vodka for you, either. Now shut the fuck up, for real."

Silence descended.

"You have any luck with Cliffy's woman?" Karolek looked up at me, raising an eyebrow as he poured the vodka again.

"Not that it's any of your concern, but no. Not yet."

"Too bad. I had hope for some progress." He handed me a glass. "Well, *Za fstrye-tchoo*." He raised his glass to me.

"*Nastrovia*."

"Not bad. You get it right."

He had me stumped. "Got what right?"

"*Nostrovia* not a toast. *Nostrovia* is a thank you for drink."

"How about that."

"How about what?" Now he was stumped.

"Never mind. We could go crazy doing the translations."

He nodded and set his glass in a cup holder.

I took the offense. "I thought you wanted me to stay out of Cliffy's business. You said you could find Felicienne."

"Maybe spoke too soon. Maybe have bigger problem."

I could feel myself slipping into the mire. "Such as?"

He said, "Maybe too many girls disappear from clubs."

"Cliffy's club?"

"Lots of clubs. Not just Sweet Mackerel."

I said, "Sounds like you need to go to Missing Persons at the police station. I told Cliffy the same thing."

"Me go to police for help? Now, that is big joke." Karolek glared at Romeo. "Don't you laugh, not that kind of joke."

"What caused you to rethink my involvement?"

"We lose valuable asset. He disappears off face of Earth."

I was confused. "He?"

"Yeah, he. Me and Romeo look all over for him. We beat up some people pretty good. Romeo excellent at getting information from folks who don't like to talk."

I could see the truth in that statement. "Who is this guy that went missing?"

"He is girly boy I pay a ton of money for. Best in class. How you call them? Trans something?"

"He's a transvestite?"

"You got it. Best in business. Blow job like you never had. I should know."

"And you bought this guy? From whom?"

"From whom? Nobody's business. Not important. Not your business."

I summed it up for him. "So, you buy a hot transvestite from persons to remain anonymous, for big bucks, and then he disappears. You were pimping this guy out?"

"Pimping out for big bucks, too. Plus, him being hot chick, he is good singer."

From behind the porno magazine Tusya chimed in. "Also, good dancer. Nice legs."

"Let me get this straight. You want me to find a talented transvestite hooker."

Karolek drained his vodka. "Yes. For me, you find my expensive good singer and dancer, talented transvestite hooker. And you do it quick. Time is money. Five thousand American dollars a night, sometimes more. Like I say, he is big asset."

"And, if I should decide this business proposition you're offering isn't something I have any interest in taking on?"

"I have Romeo beat shit out of you. Put you in hospital for long time. Okay?"

Romeo tried to cross his arms and sit up straight in the seat, but he was constrained. He settled for giving me a contented look while he mashed his right fist in his left palm.

So, that's how I got involved with human traffickers and made Margaret really upset with me.

CHAPTER 12

Tuesday morning

I still knew a small number of officers on the Portland police force who were willing to talk to me, on occasion. A few of them even traded information with me. One of the more attractive ones is Sergeant Ruth Dietz, a little gal with gorgeous red curls who could pin you to the ground and cuff you faster than you could blink. She saved my life a while back by putting a bullet in a hired killer trying to put a very long knife in me. According to the Chinese saying, once you save someone's life, you are forever in their debt. I took a chance on that being true and called her.

"Nate, it is you. When're you taking me out to dinner? Don't bring Orlando with you."

"Ruth, I've been thinking about you. It's been months since we got together."

"What a charmer, just like your jerk partner. What do you want? Do I need to save your bacon again?"

"My bacon is reasonably safe for the time being." I drew some squiggles on the note pad in front of me. "I could use some help on another matter."

"Oh, I understand. You want me to cough up some confidential information that could get me fired. Been there, done that with you."

I squiggled away. "How 'bout I ask you the question, and then you decide if I need an answer?"

"Why do I already feel like I'm in trouble? Okay, fire away."

"Missing women and girls from the skin trade, strip clubs. Maybe even vagrants."

I heard her let out a sigh. "The endless problem. Jesus, why didn't you just ask about world hunger?"

"Hit a nerve?"

"Yeah, jerk. You hit a nerve." There was a shuffling of papers at the other end of the phone. "Listen, I'm not sure I want to discuss this subject over the phone."

I put the pencil down. "Okay."

All I could hear was her breathing.

I gave her a little push. "What say you meet me tonight at *The 4th Door*, just south of Hawthorne on 35th?"

There was some hesitation. "That'll work. Nice place. I'm going to order the steak and a good bottle of wine. Bring plenty of money. That place isn't cheap."

"You're a sweetheart, Ruth."

"Don't bring Orlando."

"Got it. See you at seven thirty."

She hung up.

So, I hit a nerve. What else is new?

I looked up at the clock with the Mt. St. Helens image on the face. Donnie had picked it up when St. Helens was still a mountain.

Time to pick up Spidey.

At exactly nine thirty, I tapped on Margaret's office door. The door opened. Spidey had his hand on the knob and a smile on his face.

"Nate! Take me to school!" Lately, everything he said was followed by an exclamation point.

He spun around with the Spiderman backpack bouncing off his behind. "Bye, Mommy!" His arms went around Margaret's neck as she leaned forward in her chair. He gave her a big wet one.

"Ummmmm…" She pried his arms loose. "You be good."

I don't think I've ever seen Margaret happier.

She still had the smile when she looked up at me. "I'll pick him up at three. His lunch is in the pack along with some forms for Mrs. Saulsberry."

"I'll make sure she gets them."

The smile was still there, but it was fading fast. "And you. I want to talk to you." She stood up. "Now is not the time."

"Yeah, I know."

Spidey grabbed my hand as he flew out the door.

Margaret's words followed me down the hall. "Don't let me find out you're in this Russian mess."

CHAPTER 13

Tuesday evening

Finding a parking place on Hawthorne is similar to winning the lottery. I drove through the neighborhood on the north side for ten minutes and finally found an empty spot under a fruit tree. The street was covered with sticky reddish goo. Not relishing the idea of driving around for another half hour, I pulled to the curb. Whatever the fruit was, it was dripping. My Tacoma had suffered through worse abuse.

As I locked the driver's door and turned, two kids in ratty jeans and dirty hoodies materialized in front of me.

The shorter of the two spoke up. "Watch your car, Mister?" This was something new. I was pretty sure I hadn't taken a wrong turn and parked in South Central LA.

"What? Somebody's going to steal this old truck?"

"Never can tell, Mister."

They looked not much older than Spidey. The taller one might have been seven.

"You guys the neighborhood watch?"

They both kind of cranked their heads under their hoodies. The confused look on their faces made them look like brothers.

"Tell you what, here's a buck each." I peeled two dollars off the small roll in my pocket. "Make sure that tree doesn't drip on my truck. If it does, I'll want my money back."

The tall one pulled his hoodie back with one hand and grabbed the cash with the other. His face lit up. "Okay, Mister." They both jumped up, turned in midair, and bolted down the sidewalk to a ramshackle house.

On the porch of the house sat two young men with Rastafarian dreads and decked out in green and yellow European football jerseys. Their cigarettes looked a bit fatter than what you buy at the gas station. They were pointing at me and laughing. One of them patted the taller boy on the head and pocketed the two dollars the boy handed him.

I hollered up at the porch, "There better not be any sap on that truck when I get back."

This seemed to crack them up. Another dumb guy from the suburbs.

I gave them a good-natured thumbs up, put my hands in my pockets, and walked toward Hawthorne.

Ruth was already at the bar. A nice-looking guy in pressed jeans, an oxford shirt, and a camel blazer was hitting on her. I wondered if he had any idea she was packing heat.

Kerry, the bartender, was handing them drinks. Since Ruth was smiling, I figured there wouldn't be a need for any heroics on my part.

The guy glanced over at me when Kerry gave me a wave. Ruth reached out for my hand and pulled me in for a hello kiss on the cheek.

"Nate, this is Mitch. He works for a nuclear power company outside Chicago."

I shook his hand. "Didn't we shut down the nuclear plants out this way? Hydro is cheaper."

He nodded. "Sure, until the Columbia dries up."

"Shit, global warming does it again. You mean Trojan might get fired up again?"

He shrugged. "Not anytime soon."

I sensed someone approaching us. Casey, the hostess, had two menus and a wine list under her arm. "Mr. Harver, I have a table ready for you in the next room."

"Thanks, Casey." I took Ruth's hand and she slipped down off the stool. We said goodbye to Mitch and followed Casey through a large French door.

I pulled Ruth's chair back and commented, "He seemed like a nice guy."

"They all are, until I tell them I'm a cop."

A waiter I hadn't seen before took our drink order. A pleasant hum in the room offered the potential for an intimate romantic conversation – or one about abducted women.

Ruth studied the menu. "Well, I was going to go with the ribeye, but the salmon on the daily special menu looks good."

"I'm thinking the same thing. Let's do it. I'll get a bottle of Shea Pinot…" – a braying laugh jolted through my right ear drum. The chair behind me slammed into my back.

The laugh was followed by, "Bernie, you are too fucking much!"

The chair gave me another slam. I stood up. Ruth motioned for me to sit back down.

The guy with the potty mouth turned in his chair and looked up at me. "What's your fucking issue?"

Two other people were in the party with the jackass. One was a well-dressed black woman with a familiar face. She put her hand on the guy's forearm. "Oh, Chet. Just calm down and leave these folks to their meal."

Chet snickered in my face and turned back to the other two. The jackass was drunk. Now all three of them looked familiar to me.

Ruth gently tugged on my shirt sleeve. "Come on, Nate. Sit down. No harm done."

I settled back in my seat just in time for another horse laugh to rip through the room, followed by, "Bernie, where'd you find the ugly fucking slut you brought to the awards dinner? I thought I'd die laughing."

I turned back to their table. The couple with the jackass appeared embarrassed, but they also looked as if this was something they were used to.

As I turned back to Ruth, a general comment was bellowed to the room at large. "Who do you have to blow to get a drink in this place?"

Ruth leaned across the table. "Those three are the anchors on the six o'clock news."

I heard Casey's voice behind me. "Mr. Berkley, I'd be glad to take your drink order."

"Fuckin' A, sister. Missy, you want another Manhattan? Bernie, what do you want? Let's get a bottle of chard – oh – nay, what do ya say?" Another of his horselaughs racked the room.

Casey was embarrassed. "I'm sorry, Mr. Berkley, the room is sort of small and quiet."

"Quiet? What the fuck is your problem, sister?"

This asshole wanted to know about my issues and Casey's problems.

The chair slammed into me again. Ruth gave a sharp gasp.

I was out of my chair before Ruth could make another grab for my sleeve. Taking Chet by the nape of his neck, I plucked him out of the chair. My other hand clutched his belt from behind. We duck-marched across the room, through the French doors, and into the bar. Letting go of his neck, I opened the door to the street. Once on the sidewalk, I let him loose. He staggered around and promptly flopped onto the hood of a brand-new Mercedes.

Chet rolled over. A wet stain spread across the front of his slacks. He looked down. "I'll fuckin' sue you and the horse you rode in on, motherfucker." He slid to the pavement and got his feet caught between the front tire and the curb. His body pitched forward, hands spread out a little too late, and went face first into the sidewalk.

Missy rushed forward, trying to help him up.

Bernie came up beside me and glared down at Chet. "Stupid asshole."

Chet raised his face. He had a split lip and some good gashes on his nose and chin. "I'm calling the police, motherfucker." He wiped his hand over his bloody mouth.

Ruth was standing over Chet with her badge out. "I am the police, and you're under arrest. Drunk and disorderly. That's just for starters. Casey, do you want to press charges?"

A middle-aged woman in a black pant suit stepped in front of Casey. "We don't want any trouble here officer. Can't we just make this all go away?" She was wringing her hands.

Ruth looked at her. "Who are you?"

The hand wringing got more intense. "I'm Dotty Fisher. I'm the manager here. This is my first night. Please, can't we all calm down?"

Ruth turned to Bernie. "Get this jerk out of here. Do it now."

Bernie reached in his pocket and took out a fob. He pressed it and the Mercedes' door locks clicked open. Both he and Missy got Chet's arms and raised him to his feet. We stepped back as they maneuvered him into the back seat. Chet attempted to stabilize himself by gripping the head rest on the seat in front of him. His hands slid off and he toppled sideways.

Bernie was mumbling again. "You better not throw up, you dumb shit."

Bernie got behind the wheel. Missy got in the front and leaned between the seats, trying to get Chet rearranged in the back.

The Mercedes pulled out. It rolled slowly down the street, making a right turn on Hawthorne and then disappeared.

The crowd that had gathered drifted back into the restaurant.

Ruth grinned at me. "You really know how to show a girl a good time."

Mitch came over next to Ruth. "Nice job, officers."

Ruth smiled at him. "I'm the officer." She pointed at me. "This guy… he's just a big pain in the butt."

Walking back in the restaurant, Ruth took my arm. We stepped through the French doors and were greeted by polite applause. Within seconds everyone in the room was on their feet clapping.

Like I had told Karolek, "How about that?"

CHAPTER 14

Tuesday evening

It appeared Ruth's evening might turn out to be a good one. Somewhere amongst the applause, Mitch had managed to get Ruth's business card. I believe I heard her say, "Yes, call me."

A few minutes later, all the excitement subsided.

Dotty brought us a nice bottle of Shea Estate Pinot. When she handed me the cork she said, "Order something expensive, your meals are on us tonight."

Caesar salads arrived with anchovies, just like we asked for. Ruth had a pleasant buzz on after one glass of wine. "A little excitement helps the digestion."

I sliced up an anchovy. "You are correct, officer."

Ruth asked, "Back to business?"

"I suppose we must." I handed her the bread plate. "I hear they get this from Phillipe's Bakery."

"Sounds good. Pass the olive oil." She reached in the pocket of her jacket. "Here are some names you might find interesting."

I folded the piece of paper and laid it next to my plate. "So, my question over the phone bothered you?"

"Yeah, it bothered me. The commissioner, the mayor, the whole department are waiting for this shoe to drop."

I dipped a slice of bread in the olive oil. "That bad?"

Ruth placed her fork on her plate and sat back in the chair. "Women going missing has always been a serious citywide problem. The number of reported disappearances remained stable for years. Then, seemingly overnight, it doubled. Last year it tripled. To make it worse, the Russians and Vietnamese gangsters increased the import of slave labor, or love slaves – call them what you want. God only knows how many of them have disappeared." The arrangement of the silverware on her plate seemed to have her full attention. "Someday soon one of the newspapers or a TV station is going to wise up and figure out just how bad this situation is. You know what'll happen then."

"Proverbial heads will roll."

She took a sip of the excellent wine. "But it won't be proverbial. There'll be heads bouncing down 4th Avenue."

I don't think she even realized the wine had crossed her lips.

Casey delivered our main courses.

I picked up the slip of paper. There were two names scribbled in pencil. "Hefty Garbo? Is he still around? He must be over a hundred years old. Mickey O'Reilly? Not Mickey 'The Razor' O'Reilly? Christ, I thought he was taken out ages ago."

"We should be so lucky." Ruth took another sip of wine, this time with more interest. "A lovely meal, and it's free, and I can't even enjoy it." She shook her head. "They're retired, whatever that means in their business – porn movies, prostitution, escorts, all around human exploitation. Everything the soccer dad in Beaverton can't get at home."

I asked, "What do these two know that you don't?"

"Probably everything. We've used every law on the books to get information out of them. They won't squeal. These two didn't get to be as old as they are by ratting out their fellow miscreants." I watched my salmon cool off. "You think I can get something out of them that you can't?"

She gave me an amused look. "Donnie trained you, didn't he?"

I nodded and took a bite of the fish.

"Rumor has it that Hefty has lunch every day in the bar of The John Day Crab House on Southwest 10th. Where Hefty goes, Mickey is usually not far behind. Why don't you drop in on them in the very near future?" She started in on her fish with a vengeance.

"I've never had the pleasure of crossing paths with Mickey. It's been years since I saw Hefty. Wonder if he'll remember me?"

CHAPTER 15

Wednesday noon

He did.
The older of the two men at the table looked at me over the oxygen tube taped to his cheek. "What the fuck you want, punk?"

I said, "Hi, Hefty. Mind if I join you?"

"Fuck yes, I mind." The blue blood vessel on his translucent forehead started throbbing. "In fact, why don't you go to the dining room and get out of my fuckin' sight."

I hadn't seen anybody who looked as bad as Hefty, outside a casket, in a long time. The chair made an obnoxious screech when I pulled it out.

"Your ears broke, or what?" Mickey the Razor set his glass of beer on the table.

"Nice to meet you, Mr. O'Reilly."

The two old men looked like rejects from Madam Tussaud's Wax Museum. They were propped up, both on the same side of the table, with their backs to the wall. Old habits die hard. Neither appeared to be packing. Golf shirts hung loose from their skeletal frames.

Mickey demanded, "Who are you, you little shit bag?"

I suddenly realized Mickey was African American. At least he had some black blood flowing through the veins promenading along his shaking hands.

A gob of mashed potato dripped off Hefty's lip. "This little cocksucker plugged the clown who tried to kill Donnie Shepard a few years back. May that crazy motherfucker rest in peace."

Mickey looked confused. "Who? Shepard or the clown?"

"Both of them." Hefty wiped his lip with his napkin, smearing the potato around. He stared down at his plate looking for more potato. "Wish that psychopath had put Donnie in the ground back then. Would have saved me a lot of heartburn over the years. Shepard was the biggest pain in the ass I ever met."

I couldn't stop myself from saying, "I bet Donnie would enjoy joining us for lunch. I'm sure he's here in spirit."

My comment made Hefty jerk his head up. Another gob of mash potato rolled off his fork on to his shirt. "He fuckin' better not be here. I'd shoot the son of a bitch myself."

"You ain't got a gun anymore, Hefty." Mickey glanced down at his own emaciated chest. "Fuck, neither do I."

They both looked at me.

"I've got a .38 in an ankle holster and a nine behind me, in my belt." I reached under my jacket and moved the nine so it was more comfortable leaning back in the chair. "I'm not here to put a bullet or two in your heads. You both know you'd be dead by now if that's what I intended. No. I'm here to buy you lunch."

Hefty scowled, but Mickey smiled. "You buying lunch?" Mickey waved at the waitress. "Bring me another beer, honey."

Mickey's shaky hand reached over and gave me a pat on the arm. I'd suddenly made a friend.

Not so with Hefty. "He wants something, Razor. No such

thing as a free lunch – not from this snot-nosed piece of shit."

"Now, Hefty. My Social Security ain't arrived this month. Let's hear the young man out." Mickey looked around for the waitress. "Where's my beer?"

The waitress came around the corner with Mickey's fresh beer on a tray. "Here you go, Mickey." She had on an extremely short and tight black skirt revealing long black-nyloned legs. Her blouse was opened to show more than ample cleavage. Hefty and Mickey forgot about me and their lunch as she leaned over to hand Mickey the beer.

Hefty rolled his blue tongue around his blue lips. "If I was sixty years younger, you'd be in trouble honey."

"Well, you're not, Mr. Garbo." She flipped her order pad open and looked at me. "What'll you have, dear? Something to drink?"

"How about a HUB Pig War IPA. Oh, and I'll take the check for the table."

"Nothing to eat?"

"The beer's good. Get Mr. Garbo another drink, please."

Hefty's eyes were still firmly fixed on her open blouse. "Another gimlet, Mr. Garbo?"

"Yeah, bring him another." Mickey gave Hefty a nudge. Hefty slowly came out of his daze. "Been a while since Hefty saw anything like that. You got to excuse him."

Ignoring them, the waitress disappeared around the corner.

Mickey raised the fresh beer daintily to his lips, little finger extended. My mind spun as I recalled stories Donnie passed on to me regarding Mickey's skill wielding a straight razor with that hand. A faint film of foam glistened on his neat snow-white mustache. His other hand came up with a red cloth napkin to pat his lips dry. A class guy for a stone killer.

Mickey laid the napkin across his lap. "Well, you seem like a fine young man. What can we do for you?"

"I'd like to hear your thoughts on missing women, young women."

"Missing what, their periods?" Hefty laughed hoarsely. His face turned red and his veined palm slapped the table. The laugh became a gasp and the gasp became a rattling cough. His skull-like face grew redder as his eyes bulged. His hands gripped the table as the coughing racked what was left of a once-powerful body.

Mickey reached over and whacked his choking friend on the back. Slowly, the cough subsided, and the red face returned to a pale blue-gray pallor. Hefty sat back against the wall. "Thanks, Mick."

"I told you to stop laughing at your own jokes. You old fool. Someday I ain't going to be here, and you'll choke to death." Mickey turned back to his plate, picked up his fork, and speared a piece of asparagus.

I decided to try it again. Maybe asking enough questions would eventually kill Hefty. I'd need to be careful. "Girls disappearing from strip clubs."

Hefty waved his fork at me. "Shit. Girls been disappearing from my clubs forever, or at least trying to. They hide away enough money for a bus ticket, and their ass is gone. I ran a tight ship. Knew where every last penny was. I caught a girl holding back on me, believe me, it only would happen once. Slap the shit out of them or give them a little glimpse of Mick's razor."

Mickey nodded sagely. No need for verbal verification.

"Not like today with these Vietnamese or Russian dickheads. They couldn't line up a circle jerk, let alone a real business. Right, Mick?"

Mick gave another nod as he carefully inspected his last piece of trout for bones.

Hefty raised his gimlet glass. A confused look crossed his face. "Fuck, its empty. Where's my…?"

As if she had been waiting for just this moment, the waitress set the new drink in front of him. I noticed she had buttoned her blouse almost to the neck.

Hefty let out a breath. "About fucking time." He brought the glass up and stuck his tongue in the fizzy liquid as he drained half of the gimlet.

He looked over at Mickey. "Mick, what's the Russian's name who bought our old club out in Gresham? You know, the one that partnered up with Cliffy. What's that prick's name?"

Mickey's Alzheimer's must have been acting up. "Yeah, what was his name? Carlos something?"

Hefty was shaking his head. The clear tape holding the plastic oxygen tube pulled away from his face. He pressed it back into place. "Fuck." He made sure it was secure for the time being. "Not Carlos. Carlos was the crazy Mexican that took over the porno DVD shop in Wilsonville."

I decided to help them out. "Karolek."

Mickey set his fork on the table. "You know that hunk of rat shit?"

I nodded. "I've had the pleasure."

"Pleasure!" Hefty started laughing again. Mickey gave him another whack.

Mickey glared at him, "Told you to stop that. You want to kill yourself, do it at home." Then his gaze shifted to me. "Met his friend, the freaking giant?"

"Yes, I did."

Mickey pointed his fork at me. "Saw him take out four wet-backs Carlos sent over to northeast. Fuckin' broke them in half. Bet none of 'em ever walked again. Impressed the hell out of me."

After the meeting with Romeo in the van, Mickey's remembrance wasn't helping my self-confidence. "Some of Karolek's girls disappeared. A guy too. Cliffy's lost at least three."

Hefty got a sour look on his sour face. "That fuckin' Russian runs boys in his stable. Sick motherfucker." He looked at Mickey. "He fools grown men into thinking some gal's gobbling their knob – all the while it's a guy."

Mickey lifted his beer. "Any guy who goes in Karolek's place knows exactly what's got hold of his pecker."

Hefty feigned surprised. "What's the world coming to?"

It dawned on me I was becoming mired in an Abbott and Costello skit. "Listen, all I want to know is what you gentlemen can tell me about the surge in missing girls."

Mickey said matter-of-factly, "Somebody is takin' them and killing 'em.".

"You know this?"

He shrugged. So did Hefty.

Mickey said, "Sure. Happened before in 1955, again in '73, and then in '98. Fuckin' serial killer. Different one each time."

Hefty corrected him. "Ninety-eight was two guys."

Mickey nodded. "You're right. Two brothers."

"Watched you shoot the bald one and then slice up the skinny one."

Mickey's eyes darted around the room. "Jesus, Hefty. Not so loud."

Hefty picked up his half empty glass. "It's happening again. Just seems to roll around every twenty years or so. Like the locust coming back. Fuckin' biblical if you ask me."

Mickey pointed a manicured finger at me. "And the police ain't ever done shit to stop it. Always been up to the shop owner to handle it." He lowered his hand. "I sure as shit handled the problem in '98."

Hefty confirmed. "Sure as shit did."

CHAPTER 16

God, it feels so good.

*I*t was over. He would never have to listen to that jackass again. No more taunts in the studio, no more jabs in the bars, no more insults, no more anything.

Bernie set his leather briefcase on the rug and locked the door of his condo. Turning toward the elevator, he picked up the briefcase and thought, "God, it feels so good."

Bernie didn't even mind that the elevator stopped a half dozen times on the way to the lobby. The nice-looking babe with the orange hair from the sixteenth floor got on and said, "Good morning." to the two gay guys standing next to him. She always ignored him, but that was okay this morning.

He had decided to do himself a favor today and cab it to the studio. Getting back in his car after last night might put a damper on his mood. The smell of Chet's vomit might still be in the upholstery. After dropping Missy off, he'd pulled into Tommy's Auto Wash on Grand and scrubbed the hell out of the leather rear seat.

Fucking Chet. God, that had been sweet. Sweet and easy.

When he stepped out of the building, the sun was shining and the morning breeze smelled of fresh cut grass. He had to admit it – killing Chet had been more gratifying than sharing a girl with Rowdy at the farm. He wouldn't pass that little tidbit on to his cousin. Killing women was one thing. Now he had murdered two men. He chuckled to himself, "That, my friend, is something else."

Bernie, lost in his thoughts let two empty cabs roll by. He didn't even bother raising his arm.

Christ, it'd been so easy.

The previous evening, it was still early when he pulled the car to the curb in front of Chet's apartment building. Missy helped him get the slobbering drunk out of the backseat. The doorman took over for Missy. Bernie imagined this was a task the doorman was very familiar with.

He'd told Missy to wait in the car. The doorman was a big guy and easily maneuvered the drunken asshole to the elevator. Chet semi-sobered up, giggling all the way to the penthouse. Once there, Chet released another major upchuck when the doorman opened the door to the apartment. Bernie had shuffled the jerk to the bathroom, then turned away while Chet heaved the rest of his guts into the shower.

Bernie walked back to the front door, thanked the doorman, and handed him a fifty. Closing the door, he returned to the bathroom.

With no hesitation, Bernie strode onto the stinking marble tiled floor, lifted Chet by the back of his suit coat and belt, and with all the force he could muster slammed the sports anchor's head on the toilet bowl. The sound of Chet's skull cracking against the porcelain rim was music to Bernie's ears.

Blood flowed across the tiles. Bernie took a step backward into the hallway.

No more to do here.

He thanked the doorman again on his way through the lobby. Missy had rolled all of the windows down and was standing outside the car, fully disgusted.

On the way to Missy's house in Southeast, she bitched and moaned about the grief she put up with at the studio. All Bernie thought about was who would take over for Chet on the Sports Desk.

CHAPTER 17

Thursday morning

Wednesday evening, I'd switched off the Red Sox game about 7:30 – another benefit of living on the west coast – when Abby called to tell me she was turning off Burnside into my drive with a chilled bottle of Argyle Brut.

We managed to locate two champagne flutes and get the bottle open before we found ourselves sans clothes on the couch in the living room. Things just got better from there.

I woke up Thursday morning when Abby swung a bare leg over mine. Her morning greeting was, "Mr. Harver, don't even think about getting up."

I mumbled, "I think you've got me pinned."

"That's right." She snuggled in tight.

A couple of enjoyable minutes later she rolled back to her side the bed.

I said, "That was interesting."

Now it was her turn to mumble, "I like mornings."

I pulled the sheet up.

We were about to doze off when the alarm reminded me of the court date. In an hour and a half, the hearing would start. The thought triggered a phantom pain deep in my stomach. Being in the same room with the crazy woman who'd put several rounds from a small black pistol into me brought an ugly reality to the morning.

Regrettably, I disentangled myself from Abby. Stepping towards the door to the hallway, a pillow hit my back. The pillow was followed by, "Party pooper."

The hot water felt good. When it was turned to ice cold it felt even better. Another of life's little pleasures Molly introduced me to. Molly, Jesus, not now – not with Abby in the next room. I hadn't thought about Molly for at least a week. Maybe a world's record for me. Of all my poor choices, what I'd done to her constituted the most unforgivable series of mistakes in my life. Every time I tried to rescue our relationship, I managed to drive it further into chaos. Now she was living in New York with a restraining order against me. A mutual friend mentioned Molly might be getting married to a man she met in the city. Something else I tried not to dwell on. Well, I'd made it a week before I tripped up. Now I should set a goal for two weeks, then three, then….

"Hey, are you going to let me in there?" The shower door opened. Abby slid in between me and the shower head. "Yikes!" She jumped back out, grabbing a towel off the rack. "My God! That was cold!"

"You're trying to get me back in the sack."

She snugged the towel tight around her. "Not anymore. You've lost your chance for the rest of the morning."

I turned off the water and stepped out of the shower. "Okay. I've blown it for this morning, but what about tonight?"

She pressed up against me and brought her mouth towards mine. "Let me think about that."

MULTNOMAH COUNTY CIRCUIT COURT IS LOCATED ON

3rd Avenue near the Portland Police Station. I drove there. Art walked.

He was waiting for me on the front steps, sipping on a cup of the swill the Portland Police call coffee. "How's the tummy feeling this morning?"

"I appreciate you not bringing me a cup of that." I raised my double Americano from Courier Coffee in salute and handed him a small paper sack. "Here, got you a chocolate chip cookie."

"Thanks." He unwrapped it, took a bite, and started up the steps. "Good cookie. All is forgiven." Then he glanced over his shoulder at me. "Well, not *all* is forgiven."

Art doesn't hold grudges, but he has one hell of a long memory.

Thanks to Art and his badge, we passed through security quickly and located the assigned courtroom.

He reached for the handle on the large wooden door. "I've been shot before, and each time I faced the assailant in one of these hearings, I'd get pains from the wounds. The PPD psychiatrist told me it's not unusual."

As we walked into the courtroom, I felt another sharp pain flash through my intestines – a memory of Ms. Merriman firing the pistol from point blank range. "Something else we have in common, huh?"

"Right." He turned towards the prosecution desk in front of the Judge's bench.

I went on down the center aisle and sat in the second row. To my right sat my neighbors, the Hilgers.

Fate had stepped in and placed the Hilgers in the lobby with Ms. Merriman, Harold her bloodthirsty Shih Tzu, and me. When Ms. Merriman opened fire on me, Mr. Hilgers threw himself on her and wrenched the revolver out of her grip. For this good deed, he received a burn on his right palm from the last round fired. I'm pretty sure he saved my life. Two rounds remained in the weapon.

The Hilgers both gave me smiles and subdued waves. I nodded to them.

Art whispered something in Coleen Dodd's ear. She turned her head and gave me a look. Coleen was the prosecuting attorney on this case. For years she'd been hammering away at the worst Portland has to offer.

We all rose as Judge Ava Woods strode in. She gave me a glance that said, "Not you again". Our paths had crossed in other courtrooms.

The courtroom side door opened – the one leading to the jail. Two police matrons came through it with a prisoner between them. The person inside the orange and white striped prison uniform was unrecognizable to me. I knew it had to be Ms. Merriman, but the drawn, gray face was one I'd never seen. I remembered her as being plump. This person wasn't plump, not even close. The hair on her skull was bone-white and thinned out. The eyes nervously scanning the room were wild, rimmed in pink, and they landed right on me. The edges of her mouth turned up. A smile? Her head jerked in my direction, and she spat across the railing. One of the matrons forced her into a wooden chair behind the table. This specter who was once Ms. Merriman, swiveled her head and glared at me.

If you were to ask me what happened over the next twenty minutes, I couldn't give you many details. The prisoner was arraigned for trial. Something was said about insanity, which wasn't clear to me, but I would have agreed. Near the end, I came forward with a prepared statement when asked to do so.

I only came out of the daze when the orange prison uniform went back through the door, and it closed behind her.

Art laid a hand on my sleeve. "You okay?"

I shook my head. "Yeah. Just strange, really strange."

"It happens." He kept his hand on my arm as we walked up the aisle. "She'll spend the rest of her days in the loony bin." He shook his head. "If it hadn't been you, it would have been someone else."

"Yeah. It *was* someone else. Agent Carranzo wasn't as lucky as I was."

Art's shoulders slumped. I knew he was thinking the same thing. She could have killed Spidey along with Carranzo. We'll never completely know what happened in that basement parking lot where she fired through the window of Carranzo's El Camino.

CHAPTER 18

Friday mid-morning

The pistol jerked in Cliffy's hands. The brass ejected from the breach and bounced off the divider. We were in a booth at the Rapid-Fire Shooting Range north of town, along the Columbia River.

The target, a silhouette of a man, was hanging peacefully twenty-five feet down range. I didn't see a hole in it.

With just a hint of sarcasm, I made an observation, "I think he's still alive."

"Shit." Cliffy rearranged his stance. He gripped the Smith and Wesson M&P9 with both hands, let out a breath, and squeezed the trigger just like I'd shown him. The sound of the shot echoed around the range. The target remained at peace.

I tugged my earmuffs down. "When's the last time you fired a gun?"

"Never." He laid the pistol on the wooden shelf.

"You're kidding? You've never fired a gun?"

He shook his head. "Why do you think I wanted you to bring me here?"

"Let's try it again." I snugged my earmuffs back on.

This trip to the range, I suspected, was an attempt by Cliffy to regain some of his manhood or assuage his self-presumed guilt for Felicienne's disappearance.

Four shots later, the paper target swayed when the figure on it took a graze along its right shoulder.

A sly smile curled Cliffy's lip. "I wounded the motherfucker."

"He's probably left handed, and we're both dead now." I handed Cliffy a fresh magazine with only six rounds in it. "Just keep in mind; if you've fired two rounds at the guy and he's still standing, he's probably standing over your dead body."

"That's not very reassuring."

"It's not meant to be. Now, put the fresh magazine in and do it again."

We emptied a box of fifty bullets. I retrieved the target for the last time and counted twenty holes in it. Fourteen in the orange body, and four of those in the 7 and 8 slots of the bulls-eye. None in the center. One round went through the right side of the silhouette's head. It could have been worse.

"You've got some work to do." I handed Cliffy the broom. "Sweep up your brass and put them in the red bucket."

I opened the handgun case Cliffy bought earlier that morning. The S&W fit snugly inside. He would need some instruction on cleaning the weapon. I held out hope for him. This may have been the first time I'd seen anything hold his interest for longer than a couple of seconds. Well, other than Felicienne.

When we exited the range through the gun shop, Maxine was behind the counter. I gave her a wave. Maxine had worked the strip club circuit a few years back. Cliffy told me she was one of the best in the trade.

She asked, "How did he do, Nate?"

"Time will tell. I want him in here twice a week until we see some holes in the center." I opened the door to the parking lot. "Let me know if he doesn't show up."

"Will do. Say hi to Molly. Haven't seen her in ages."

That stung. Hard to believe there were still people we'd know who weren't aware our story was long over.

Cliffy climbed into the passenger's seat of my Tacoma. "I need to tell you something." He reached for the seat belt. "Karolek lost another girl."

"When did this happen?"

"Yesterday afternoon he realized she was gone."

"Thursday?" I turned the ignition over.

"Yeah. Name's Gisele. She didn't show up for the lunch crowd. He sent Romeo over to the apartment she was sharing. The other girl told him Gisele left for work before noon. Romeo checked the apartment. Her stuff was still there."

I pulled out of the parking lot onto Marine Drive. "So, she disappeared somewhere between the apartment and the club?"

Cliffy said, "Five blocks. Karolek likes to keep the girls close to work."

"It was broad daylight, right? Nobody saw anything?"

Cliffy's voice was dry, and I doubted it was from the gun smoke. "Will you take a look, Nate? Romeo might be able to break me in half, but he can't find his ass with both hands."

"I'll see what I can turn up." I accelerated up the entry ramp to Interstate 5 and merged with the traffic heading into Portland.

When I dropped Cliffy off at The Sweet Mackerel, construction of the new building was going full bore. Walls were going up. Carpenters and laborers were hard at it.

Cliffy slid out of the passenger's seat and gently closed the door. Through the open window he said, "Felicienne's dream is taking shape."

CHAPTER 19

Friday noon

Traffic was sparse along Powell Boulevard on the drive across town. Just after I turned south onto SE Foster Road, I found Karolek's club. The brown concrete block building looked like it could use a sand blasting and a fresh coat of paint. The Nude Dancers sign looked a little grimy.

I parked a block away and walked back to the club. The surrounding neighborhood was industrial – or had been. Barbwire was stretched along the top of high chain-link fences enclosing most of the businesses. Several of the buildings appeared to be abandoned.

Cliffy told me the missing girl's apartment building was five blocks east and on the opposite side of the street. Walking east from the club, I looked across the street at the route I assumed Gisele had taken. There were no residential buildings. The girl's apartment building was the first structure that could be considered housing – not exactly the kind of housing I'd want to live in. Two blocks west of the apartment on the same side of the street was a break in a fence. Several feet of chain-link had been pulled back providing an opening to an asphalt lot. On the property and about fifty feet back from the fence, a piece of blue plastic tarp hung against a dilapidated corrugated steel building. The tarp formed a half-tent. Shelter for someone?

Shards of broken glass, rusting cans, rotting pieces of wood, and what I hoped was solidified dog shit, covered the humped ground in front of me. A pile of rags rested against the side of the building just outside the blue tarp.

The pile moved as I walked to it. A green bottle came out of the rags. Attached to the bottle was a hand covered with a red rash. Walking closer, I could make out the side of a face, the bottle tipped up to its lips. The bottle, hand, and face disappeared back into the rags.

I waved. "Hello."

The pile shrunk and began to quiver. Two rotting leather boots slipped out from under it and trembled against the asphalt. The head appeared again and turned to rest against the side of the building.

From under the blue tarp a filthy red and black Trailblazer's ball cap darted out and then shot back inside. "Fuck off!"

I was pretty sure it was a female voice, maybe a child.

"I'd like to talk to you." I looked around. Then I took out my wallet and found a ten-dollar bill. "I can give you money."

Nothing happened. The pile of rags might have gotten a bit smaller. The quiver was still going.

Thirty seconds may have passed. Then, "What you want?"

"Just to talk. I'm looking for someone."

"Nobody's here."

"No, they were out on the street." I looked at the bill in my fist. "There's ten bucks here. Let's talk for a minute."

The Blazers cap crept back out. The face under it glared at me. It was female.

She looked toward the pile of rags. "Don't fuck with Caboose. Okay?"

I looked down at the pile. "That's Caboose?" There had to be a story there.

"Yeah." She barked at me. "Don't come any closer. I got a knife."

"Do you want the money or not?"

She gave me a weak, "Okay", and crawled out from under the tarp.

When she stood up her dirty green parka seemed to weigh her down. She might have been five feet tall. She wasn't a child. Her face was scarred. The skin had been peeled off both cheeks. It looked as though someone had taken sandpaper to it.

She held out her hand. A green and white mitten with Santa Claus figures opened. "Give me the money."

With my arm outstretched, I took three steps toward her. She snatched the bill from my fingers.

"Are we good now?" Trying to look nonthreatening, I put my hands into the pockets of my jeans.

The ten vanished into the parka and she nodded.

"I'm looking for a woman who may have disappeared from this area yesterday." I turned and pointed to the street behind me.

"Nooooooo!" A flash of steel appeared in the Santa Claus mitten. She fell back against the building and slid down against Caboose. "Get away. I'll stick you, goddam you. I'll stick you." She jerked the blade up at me.

I stepped back. "I'm not going to hurt you."

"Where is he?" Her eyes darted around the yard. "Where is he? I'll fucking stick you good. Where is he?"

"Where is who?"

"The big fucker…" A sob cut her off. She dropped the blade. Her hands were shaking so badly she couldn't pick it back up. "Oh, Jesus!" She wrapped herself around the pile of rags. An arm came out of the pile and wrapped around her. The sobbing went on and on.

I said, "It's just me. There's no one else. Here, look around."

She looked up. Tears streaked the grime and raw flesh on her cheeks. "Who are you?"

"Just a guy looking for a girl. She may have been abducted by someone bad."

"That's what the big guy wanted." At least the crying had subsided.

"Was this guy real tall, long black hair, big leather coat? Smelled like Brut?"

Her face tightened. "Yeah. He fuckin' stank."

"Romeo."

"Who?"

"Never mind. He asked about the girl, too?"

She wiped her nose with the Santa Claus mitten. "He asked Caboose. Caboose don't talk so good. He wouldn't know anything anyway. He ain't right."

"Tell me what happened with Rom… the big guy."

"He was pokin' Caboose. Asking him shit. Caboose don't understand. The guy kicked Caboose. Kicked him a bunch – and hard too."

"He hurt you?"

"The guy was kickin' Caboose and saw me under the tarp. He grabbed me and tried to pull me out. I cut him with my knife. Only got his coat. Then he went nuts. Got hold of my head and scraped my face on the asphalt. Stomped my back with his boot. "

I squatted down. "Did he ask you about the girl?"

"Yeah, finally. He got done kickin' me and then he wanted to know if I saw a girl get grabbed."

"Did you?"

"I didn't tell that motherfucker nothing. It hurt too bad to talk. The son of a bitch."

Standing up, I took my wallet out again. This time I took out two twenties.

Her eyes got big. She pried herself off Caboose and stood up.

I held the two bills pressed along my leg. "Did you? Did you see something?"

"Yeah." She wiped her nose again. "I saw her get snatched."

CHAPTER 20

Friday afternoon and evening

Ruth drove up in a light brown Chevy Impala and parked next to the hole in the fence. She got out of the car, opened the back door, bent down, and reached in. When she stood up, there were two Burgerville bags in her arms and two cans of Diet Coke in her jacket pockets. She wore her civvies – jeans with a blue Patagonia windbreaker. Her black combat boots didn't seem to mind the broken glass and garbage.

I turned back to Caboose and the woman. "Here comes my friend Ruth. She needs to hear what you told me."

The woman was squinting under her Blazer's hat. A smile curled her lips. "She's got burgers, Caboose." She reached down and tugged on the pile of rags. "Sit up. We got real burgers."

Somehow the pile of rags righted itself.

Ruth walked up next to me and looked at the woman and Caboose. "Nate."

"Thanks, Ruth." I took the bags from her.

After the woman peeled off her gloves, I handed her the bags. Sitting down next to Caboose, she put one in his hands and ripped hers open.

Ruth passed me the Cokes. I set them down in front of Caboose.

The woman finished off one burger and started in on the second. "Good." Her mouth was full, but she got the word out.

All I could tell about Caboose was that both of his burgers had disappeared.

Ruth nodded to me and we stepped out of earshot.

Ruth looked doubtful. "She saw someone take the girl? She's sure? We hear a lot of things from homeless people when they think they can get something."

"No. I think she saw it happen. Caboose is pretty well out of it, but not her."

Ruth looked back at the pair. "God, I hope you're right."

"She said an old black Ford van was parked by the curb with the side door pulled back. The driver stood outside for a long time drinking out of a bottle. The girl came down the street and walked by the van. The driver grabbed her and tossed her in."

Ruth shook her head. "It all sounds pretty brazen to me. Right here in broad daylight?" She looked out on the street.

"There's some traffic. Not a lot. No pedestrians to speak of." I pointed up Foster Boulevard. "The van would have blocked the view. So simple it worked."

Ruth shivered and shook her head. "Jesus." She folded her arms around herself. "She's sure it was a Ford van and it was black?"

"Says she knows her cars. Hell, maybe she does. Said it was a late model. A mismatched wheel on the rear-driver's side. One of those cheap black ones."

"And the driver?"

"Tall white guy, white coveralls, brown straw hat. Clean-shaven, about forty, maybe fifty."

Ruth turned and watched the woman for a few seconds.

"She's probably on something. We could give her a blood test. Need her consent." Ruth paused and shook her head. "I just don't know."

We walked back to the building. Lunch was over. The bags were crumpled and tossed aside.

The woman was finishing one of the Cokes. I didn't see the other one. Caboose must have hidden it.

Ruth squatted down in front of her. "What's your name?"

"Ruth Ann. Just like you. Almost." She smiled at us and for an instant I saw a pretty face that must have lived there a long, long time ago.

Ruth extended her hand to Ruth Ann. "I'd like to get a statement from you." She paused for a moment before adding, "We need you to come downtown to do it."

Ruth Ann squirmed up against Caboose. "I don't know about that. You going to keep me there? Lock me up? What about Caboose? I can't just leave him."

"No, you won't have to stay. You've done nothing wrong."

"I'm squatting on this property. You can arrest me." The tears were coming again.

"We're not going to arrest anybody, except the creep who took the girl."

Now she was really scared. "What about the big guy. He gonna come back and beat us again for talking to the cops?"

I said, "No. I'll take care of him. He's not coming back."

Ruth gently placed her hand on Ruth Ann's sleeve. "Can you trust us?"

Ruth Ann raised her arm and put her hand on the pile of rags. "What about Caboose? You take him in, somebody's gonna see how messed up he is and put him away somewhere?" The tears were flowing.

Ruth looked up at me with a question in her eyes.
I shrugged.

That's how I ended up spending the rest of the day and most of the night sitting next to Caboose on the cold asphalt. He wasn't much of a conversationalist.

CHAPTER 21

Saturday morning

Spending the evening scrunched up against a steel building isn't my idea of a fun Friday night.

Now the sweat was pouring out of me, and the muscles in my back and legs had stopped aching. Orlando and I ran down the hill on the south side of the cemetery and sprinted across Burnside Road. Two more laps through the tombstones to go. Then we'd start on the stairs.

A few days in LA had done Orlando a world of good. The rain and sleet threatening the grape harvest had miraculously missed the Willamette Valley. His mood had certainly improved. I wondered what else might have contributed to his enhanced disposition. Could be he got lucky in LA. Orlando is pretty damn discreet. He just gets more sociable when he's spent some quality time with one of his female acquaintances. The new layer of gravel on the maintenance road north of the cemetery was making my feet slip. I concentrated on my balance. Orlando had just jumped over on the grass when I heard truck tires squeal behind us. Over my shoulder I saw dust swirl around a huge Mercedes 6x6 Desert Beast. It accelerated up the gravel road straight at us. I sprang to the left. Orlando summersaulted to the right.

By the time I got to my feet, I had the Derringer out of my hip pocket. The big-ass truck had spun around in a cloud of dust and gravel. I saw something black in Orlando's hands spitting flame as he dove behind a large tombstone. He never left the house unarmed either.

The Mercedes braked hard and slewed in my direction. Both tires on the driver's side were blown. Nice shooting on Orlando's part. The tires on the passenger's side slid into a freshly dug trench. The truck flipped on its side plowing up a hundred feet of sod as it slid down the hill.

Orlando and I sprinted down the hill, pistols gripped and pointed at the driver's window. We stood a good twenty feet apart as the truck came to a halt.

Mud covered the hood and windshield. Romeo's big head poked through the open driver's window. He was all smiles as he agilely hoisted himself up through the window. Behind him, Karolek crawled out not quite as gingerly, and definitely not smiling.

Karolek looked at us. As he steadied himself, he appeared to be registering the fact there were guns pointed at him. Romeo was unfazed and didn't seem to give a shit as he took a step toward Orlando. Orlando fired into the ground between Romeo's feet. That stopped the giant.

Romeo turned his attention to me. "So, you going to shoot me with little piss-ant pop gun? Huh?"

I aimed at his chest. "It's a .45. It'll blow your fucking leg off. Or your head. Your choice."

Karolek gave Romeo a hard shove. "You are dumb shit. Shut the fuck up."

He stepped from behind Romeo and motioned to me. "Why the fuck you shoot at us? Now truck all fucked up. We only want to talk."

Orlando had Romeo covered, so I shifted the barrel of the Derringer to Karolek. "Okay. You've got my attention. Talk to me."

"Why you not tell Karolek you find witness?" He really looked disappointed. "We have deal."

I pointed the weapon back at Romeo. "The deal I recall was that this asshole was going to beat the shit out of me if I didn't do what you told me to."

"Still." Karolek shrugged. "I need information to find motherfucker who takes my property."

I was starting to get pissed off. "Your property is a living breathing human being. A young woman."

"No, just whore."

God, did I ever want to shoot him. "You make me want to puke."

"Why? Just business. Karolek out a bunch of cash if girl doesn't turn up."

I couldn't find the words. I lowered the Derringer to the ground between us. But Orlando kept his pistol leveled on Romeo's chest. "The witness?"

This caught Romeo's attention.

Karolek put his hands on his hips. "Yeah, the witness. Why homeless witness talk to you and not Romeo?"

"I'd say it was because I gave them some money. And, I didn't start beating the shit out of a sick man and a woman before I started asking questions."

Karolek turned to Romeo. "You do that?"

"Sure. Usually work. Save time." Romeo seemed quite proud of his strategy.

Karolek took a swing at him. Romeo took the blow and stepped back a foot or so. He looked like a kid who just got cuffed by his old man.

Karolek shook his head. "Running a business in this country not easy."

Three maintenance men, rapidly firing off replies to one another in Spanish, were jogging up the gravel road toward us. A very pale over-weight guy was trying to keep up with them. They wore bright orange and yellow reflector vests.

The fat guy must have been the supervisor. He stopped in front of the Mercedes swearing under his breath. He tilted his head in our direction while pointing at the overturned truck. "Who does this piece of crap belong to?"

Nonchalantly, I slipped the Derringer back in my hip pocket. Orlando's piece had disappeared as well. I smiled at Karolek. "Well, in the words of Ricky Ricardo, 'Looks like you got some splainin' to do, Lucy.' Good luck asshole."

Orlando and I took off at an easy pace down the gravel road.

CHAPTER 22

Saturday afternoon

I turned the key in my office door. Behind me, the door to the stairs groaned open. Next came the sound of footsteps, and I slid my hand inside my jacket. The brief business meeting with Karolek had me skittish.

A female voice behind me said, "You won't need that gun."

"Sorry, Ruth." I released the grip on the pistol, turned the knob, and swung the door open. Stepping back, I waved her in. "Ladies first."

"Always the gentleman." She stepped into the office.

"Coffee, tea, or me?" Such was my weak attempt to lighten the mood after almost pulling a gun on her.

"Definitely not the latter. Some of Orlando's finest tea? By the way, you seem a little jumpy this morning."

I nodded, "Had a stressful jog through the cemetery. Crazy guy in a Mercedes van almost ran over me. Oh, and you'll be glad to know Orlando's due to show up in an hour or so." I opened the cupboard and took out a tin of Orlando's best.

"I'll make it a point to get out of here before then."

No love lost between those two.

"How'd the statement go with Ruth Ann?"

"God, that poor woman." Ruth dropped her windbreaker on the table in front of the couch. "My heart was breaking when I dropped her off on Foster last night."

"Yeah, I gave her another twenty before I left them."

"Jeez, not much of a *thank you* for doing her civic duty after some thug tried to scrape her face off and beat her to a pulp." Ruth wrapped her arms around her shoulders.

I turned on the heat under the tea kettle. "You've got a horse-shit job. You know that?"

"No kidding, Sherlock." She sat down on the couch.

"Any luck tracking the van?"

"Not yet. Too early to expect anything on that, if ever." She settled in with her legs under her.

"Want a blanket?"

Her eyes were focused on a spot somewhere out the window. There was nothing on the other side of the street but a brick wall. "Yes. That would be nice."

I found a wool blanket in the closet and handed it to her. By the time she was wrapped up and comfy, the tea kettle let us know the water was ready. I set a tea strainer with some of Orlando's Oriental Beauty in a pot and poured in water. "Lemon and honey?"

"Straight up, if you would."

"No problemo."

I brought cups and the pot to the table. "Let's let it steep for a couple of minutes."

"If you tell anyone I let you cuddle me, I will kick your ass."

"It'll be our secret."

We sat comfortably, sipping our tea, and looking at each other for a few minutes.

Ruth put her teacup down on a year-old copy of *Portland Monthly*. "I got the okay to stake out a handful of strip clubs for the next couple of weeks. Want to see if any black Ford vans show up."

I said, "You know we have more than a handful of strip clubs in town. Throw in Gresham, Beaverton and Hillsboro and there's a ton more. What about McMinnville, or Salem, or Bend?"

She tugged the blanket tighter. "Yeah. Needle in a haystack. But I've got to do something."

The door opened and Orlando stepped in. He had one arm out of his jacket before he saw Ruth. An awkward few seconds elapsed.

Orlando said, "Hi."

"Hi, to you." She sat up. The blanket slipped off her shoulders. "Guess I'll head back to the station."

Orlando hung his jacket over the back of his chair. He walked to the wall and leaned back against it.

Ruth collected her bag and opened the door. "I'll keep in touch. Ruth Ann agreed to contact me if she remembers any more about the van, or the guy in it."

I said, "Okay. Guess I'll see you when I see you."

"Right." She smiled at me, letting her glance fan across Orlando as she went out the door.

We listened to her steps retreat down the hallway tile. The door to the stairs opened and closed.

I turned to Orlando. "Well, that was just a tad uncomfortable. Didn't expect you to show up for another hour of so."

He shrugged. "For a while there, we were the best. Then, we were the worst. I don't understand it."

"Nobody does."

I went to my desk. He turned around and stared out the window at the same brick wall Ruth had been watching.

CHAPTER 23

Sunday morning

Sunday morning, they found Felicienne's body.

By *they*, I mean the two electricians pulling wires in a small crawlspace under the new kitchen at the Sweet Mackerel. They'd installed high-wattage temporary lighting under the floor. One of the electricians, on his hands and knees running conduit along the east wall, saw something sticking out of the foundation. It took him a few seconds to figure out it was a finger. When he did, he lost his breakfast and Saturday night's dinner. Art was fairly sure the upchuck would not make forensics' job any easier.

To make matters worse Cliffy had been in the old club reading the New York Times Sunday edition and having his morning coffee. Since none of the girls were around and Karolek and crew were not early risers, Cliffy was alone when the two electricians ran into the bar yelling in Spanish.

Cliffy couldn't understand them and crawled down into the space for a look-see. The finger had the remnants of a purple shade of nail polish dusted with gold flakes.

According to the electricians, Cliffy went *jodidamente loco*, which I'm pretty sure means *fucking crazy*. They said Cliffy began screaming. He grabbed a 14-pound sledgehammer pounding it into the crawlspace wall.

One of the electricians got smart and dialed 911.

When the responding officers arrived, Cliffy was covered in concrete dust, mud, and his own blood. Getting him out of the crawl space could not have been an easy task.

When Art arrived, Cliffy was rolling around in the gravel parking lot screaming for someone to call me. When I got there, I found him sitting in the back of a squad car, cuffed, filthy, and sobbing.

I looked at Art. "You cuffed him?"

"The responding officers did. He was berserk. Still is."

There were three squad cars and two unmarked vehicles in the parking lot. An ambulance pulled in and parked over by a resting backhoe.

Art told one of the other officers to remove the cuffs. After a few minutes, the paramedics helped Cliffy out of the backseat and into the ambulance.

Another officer was running crime scene tape around the area.

Art wandered over to the east side of the new kitchen.

I followed him. "What are you going to do?"

Art squatted down and peered through the opening into the crawlspace. "Rip it down. Carefully. May take a while." He stood up. "Between the electricians and Cliffy the crime scene is pretty well contaminated."

The sweatshirt he wore said *World's Greatest Dad*. I think Margaret picked it out for Spidey to give to him on his birthday. "We'll need to spend some quality time with Cliffy down at headquarters. Can't say I'm looking forward to that this afternoon."

"You mind if I speak with Cliffy?"

"Okay." Art looked over at the ambulance. "If you get a confession out of the jerk, call me over."

"Art, that wasn't called for."

He shrugged and nodded his head. "Point taken."

I guess I can't blame Art. He hadn't had the opportunity to spend time with the new and improved Cliffy.

Turning around, I saw a tall silver-haired man in a black raincoat with his back to me staring into the ambulance. He was watching Cliffy. Cliffy didn't seem to be aware of the man.

I felt a chill jump up my spine and a tremble start in my right hand. Taking a step forward became an impossible task. My lungs weren't taking in oxygen.

Donnie was only a couple of feet in front of me. He turned and faced me. His hands were on his hips holding the raincoat open. His old Army Colt .45s was jammed in his belt. One of the responding officers walked behind Donnie like he wasn't even there. The officer gave me a wave. I remembered him from a cookout at Art's house.

Donnie said, "Let this asshole wallow in his own special hell. He was a piece of shit, still is, and always will be."

I shook my head. "No, Donnie. I can't."

"You can't? What the fuck do you mean, *you can't*?"

"Things have changed, Donnie."

"With Cliffy, nothing ever changes. I had ample opportunity to rid the world of him and didn't. Major mistake on my part."

Watching me, the officer walked to his squad car. He had a strange expression on his face.

"You're dead, Donnie. I love you, but you're dead. You need to stay that way." I walked toward the rear of the ambulance.

Over my shoulder I heard Donnie's words as his voice faded away. "You're gonna regret this."

CHAPTER 24

Monday afternoon

It took most of Sunday to get Felicienne's body parts, all fourteen of them, removed from the foundation. Still, the police weren't sure they had them all.

Art sent several of his people out to collect Karolek and his crew. Not all of them came peacefully. Two of the homicide detectives ended up with broken bones when they tracked down Romeo at a second-run movie theater in Happy Valley. He was watching a special showing of *Frozen*. Art told me he had the same problem with Spidey and the movie – only on a smaller scale.

So far, five different construction crews had worked on the construction site. Art rounded all of them up, except for a crew of HVAC guys on a job in the San Juan Islands.

Everyone involved with the Sweet Mackerel was interviewed, including the girls and the janitors. A Portland PD detective came across the birthdates of two of the strippers. That threw the investigation into a whole new realm of mayhem. Family Services joined the investigating team.

Art didn't get his wish. No confession came from Cliffy. Cliffy went comatose – incapable of responding to anything, let alone questioning.

Thanks to the underage strippers, Cliffy did find himself behind bars. A few attorneys in town specialize in the services Cliffy required, and one of them was hard at work getting him bailed out.

At 5:00 that afternoon, I drove out to pick up Spidey for his weekly parkour lesson. It's the only activity Spidey liked more than our Playdate PDX adventures.

Margaret was tugging an OSU Beavers sweatshirt over his head when he swung their front door open.

"Too tight, Mommy!"

"Just hold on for a sec, mister." She got his arms through the sleeves. When she pulled it down, he had an inch of tummy showing above his belt. "Is this kid ever going to stop growing?"

"I'll stop at Target and pick up a couple of bigger sweatshirts." I took his hand.

"Get the cheap ones. He'll outgrow them in a month."

"Eating dinner alone tonight?"

"Yes, and for several to come. Art will be forever sorting through that strip club…," She glanced at Spidey. "…situation. How well did you know her?"

"I met her a few times. She wasn't what you would expect, knowing Cliffy. Sometimes matters of the heart can't always be explained."

"Art is betting on Cliffy for the culprit."

Spidey was tugging on my arm. I nodded, "Yeah, him and Donnie."

"What?"

Jeez, what was the matter with me?

"I meant, Art and a bunch of other people."

Margaret gave me a confused look. "Have him home before 7:00 tonight. Oh, and no stopping at you-know-where."

No Twist yogurt for Spidey tonight. "And, I had my heart set on a Cookies N' Cream."

Spidey gave me another tug. "Twist, Nate?"

Margaret pushed us out the door. "Now you've done it. Sugar-free. Do you hear me? Sugar-free."

Spidey was a happy guy as we bounded down the steps and out to my truck.

CHAPTER 25

Tuesday morning

Sergeant Thurmond walked me into Art's office and pulled the door closed behind us.

Art was sitting straight up in his chair with his arms tightly crossed over his chest. His tie was scrunched up under his chin. He didn't seem to notice. He was really pissed off.

Across the desk sat Karolek, quite at ease. He waved a hand dismissively in the air. "What you want me to do? Confess? Bullshit, Mr. Detective."

Art pointed at me. I think I heard his teeth grind. "You and Thurmond have a seat." He returned his attention to Karolek. "This piece of shit claims you're working for him."

His hands spread in dismay, Karolek's eyes grew even larger. "Detective, why you treat me this way? I am here of free will." His hands dropped to his knees. The look of consternation remained on his face. "I want only to help."

Art glared at Karolek but spoke to me. "Care to explain?"

I, too, was there to help. "Nothing to explain. Our friend here asked me to look into the disappearance of a couple of his employees. I believe I left him with the impression I'd think about it but to not hold his breath."

The hands were up again. "Why hold breath, private investigator? We have understanding."

"The only thing I understood was the Incredible Hulk would use me for a punching bag." I looked around the room. "Where is Romeo? Heard he upset a bunch of five-year-old kids when the police hauled him out of a Disney movie."

Art mumbled, "He's experiencing Portland PD hospitality in a holding cell – assaulted two of our officers."

Karolek smirked. "We see about that. Romeo peacefully watching movie when policemen attack him. Cause him great pain and discomfort. Not even brutality like that in Russia." He shrugged. "Well, maybe some."

"Thurmond, show this Cossack asshole out of here." Art got up. "Meeting over."

Karolek's chair made a sound like fingernails on a blackboard when he scooted it back. He stood at attention. "Cossacks strong Russian fighters. None of them *assholes*. You need to study history book, Mr. Detective." He saluted Art, turned, gave me the evil eye, and walked out the door.

Thurmond was on the move before the door closed behind Karolek.

I stood up and walked to the window. A small piece of the Willamette River was visible between the two buildings across the street. "You guys have a chance to look into the two other girls who went missing from the Sweet Mackerel?"

"We don't have any records of missing persons reports being filed. Do you have their names?"

"Cliffy will have them. I don't think there's anybody left at the Sweet Mackerel over twelve to ask." I turned around. "Is he still in custody?"

Art checked his watch. "No. I believe the esteemed Mr. Hasick made bail a little over an hour ago." He looked at me. "That reminds me, I'll need to get his cell fumigated."

"Want me to get the missing girls names and addresses for you?"

"No. That's called police work. Am I correct in assuming you haven't joined the force in the last few minutes?"

"Only trying to make myself useful."

"I'm the world's expert on what happens when you make yourself useful. Why don't you follow Thurmond to the front door?" He opened a file and started flipping through it.

I walked out the door.

CHAPTER 26

Tuesday afternoon

As it turned out, there was someone over twelve years of age at the Sweet Mackerel. She was giving a piece of her mind to the police officers blocking her way.

"My shit is in there!" The iridescent purple wig on her shaved head had slipped back. The tattoo of a blue bird was partially visible.

"This is a crime scene, lady. You need to step back." The police officer was the same one I'd met at Art's cookout, the same one who caught me talking to Donnie. He looked at me. "Harver, same goes for you."

The girl adjusted her wig and pulled a hoodie up over her head. "My only coat is in there. Give me a fucking break." She pulled the sweatshirt tighter around herself.

"Can't help you. Check downtown tomorrow morning. Maybe the crime team will release it." He pointed to me. "What do you want?"

"Just looking for Cliffy."

"Well, Cliffy isn't here." Then, to both me and the girl, "Go back to your vehicles."

I know when to beat a retreat. Shrugging my shoulders, I pulled my hoodie up too. The fine mist that filled the air was turning to rain.

The girl was a few feet in front of me, struggling through

the deep ruts left by the earth movers and trucks. I figured she stood a good chance of turning an ankle in her high heels before she made it to the sidewalk.

I grabbed her arm just as a heel snapped off and she tumbled forward. "I've got you."

She tumbled against me. "Oh, shit!" Tears filled her eyes. "My Nikes are in there too."

"Is your car here?" I looked around, but the only vehicle nearby was my pickup.

There was a tremor in her voice. "I took the bus."

"Do you want a lift?"

Her eyes darted at me. "How do I know you're not a creep?"

"There are a few folks in town who would rally to confirm your fears."

"Huh?"

"Let's just say I'm here, trying to help Cliffy."

"You a friend of Cliffy's?"

"In a way, yes."

She shook her head. "Then you *are* a creep."

"Okay, you want a ride or not?"

She looked down Sandy Boulevard toward town. The nearest bus stop was a couple of blocks away. "Yeah, but keep your hands to yourself. I ain't working."

I helped her over the last of the ruts. When we got in the cab, I reached behind the seat, grabbed an old wool blanket, and handed it to her.

She mumbled, "Thanks".

The traffic on Sandy was hardly moving. I finally spotted a break, pulled out crossing the east-bound lane, and made a quick turn to the west. "Where do you live?"

She pulled the blanket snugly around her. Staring out the passenger's window, she said, "Forest Grove."

"Forest Grove! You took the bus here from Forest Grove?"

She nodded. "A bunch of them."

"That's how you get to work? You take buses from Forest Grove all the way out here?"

She sulked, tugging the hoodie tighter around her head. "What the fuck we supposed to do? Walk?" She turned her face back to the window.

I was confused. "We? What do you mean *we*?"

"Me and Rowena."

Rowena? I steered to the side of the road and stopped. "Rowena. Wasn't she the girl who disappeared? Disappeared around the same time as another girl, just before Felicienne?"

"Yeah. Why did you pull over? Don't get any ideas." Her hand was on the door handle. Her eyes were nervous.

"Sorry." I checked the mirrors and pulled into the westbound traffic.

I drove to 33rd Avenue, taking the ramp to Interstate 84 West heading to the Sunset Highway.

"Why did you ask about Rowena?" She was watching the traffic in front of us.

"Cliffy told me Felicienne had gone looking for her. Shortly afterwards, Felicienne went missing."

"I liked Felicienne. Felicienne understood us. Everybody else thinks we're just a bunch of dumb strippers or thinks we're hookers. I ain't no hooker. Maybe once or twice I took some money to go out in the parking lot. But only a couple of times. Rowena only did it cuz she needed money for her kid." She squeezed her arms around her shoulders. "Her brother, Jerry, caught her in a guy's car one night. Jerry used to drive us here from Forest Grove and pick us up. God, he slapped the shit out of her that night. Stopped giving us the ride, too. That's how we ended up taking the bus."

And, I thought I had problems. "Sorry."

"What you got to be sorry for? That dipshit Jerry is the one should be sorry. Called us the whores of baboon."

"Baboon? You mean Babylon?"

"Yeah, maybe. He is one big Jesus freak. He'd preach to us while he drove us to work. If Rowena's mom hadn't insisted, he would've never driven us." She let out a slobbery laugh. "Course, once he caught Rowena with that nasty old guy, he wasn't driving us, no matter what her mom said."

"When was it that Jerry caught Rowena?"

"Couple of days before she disappeared."

My mind was spinning. "Does Jerry live with his mother?"

"Nah. Not anymore. I heard he got work at a construction site up in Bellingham."

"What's he do?"

"Pours concrete, or something."

CHAPTER 27

Tuesday evening

When I exited The Sunset Highway at Forest Grove, I made the assumption she was hungry. I also figured she knew more about what was going on than I did.

We pulled into a Chinese restaurant on Pacific Avenue, and I bought her dinner. She scooped down a full appetizer of Crab Rangoon, a bowl of sweet and sour soup, a plate of General Tao's chicken, rice, and half of my eggplant with garlic sauce. The large Coke she washed it down with disappeared into her tiny stomach.

Somewhere between the soup and the chicken, she told me her name was Gale, but her working name was "Stitches". When I inquired about that, she pulled back her wig and showed me a long scar that wrapped around her shaved head. That was when I offered her the rest of my eggplant. The scar was the result of a conversation she had with her ex-boyfriend, just before he shipped out to Afghanistan.

She slurped down the last of her Coke, sighed, and told me Jerry's last name was Finnegan. I thumbed a note into my iPhone.

I dropped her at a trailer park on the south side of town. She thanked me and actually shook my hand before getting out of the truck. I watched her walk down the gravel road between the trailers. Two chained-up dogs barked, until they recognized her. She turned right, looked back at me, and waved. Then she disappeared.

I sat there a few minutes with the motor running, thinking about what Gale told me. Then I drove back to Forest Grove and pulled into the parking lot of a grocery store. I called Art.

"Nate, I'm walking out the door. Spidey's making demands on Margaret for a Hotlips' ham and pineapple pizza tonight. No doubt, something you introduced into his diet."

"Hey, I just got some information from one of Cliffy's girls. Should interest you." I watched an elderly Asian woman push a grocery cart bigger than she was across the gouged-up asphalt lot.

"If I recall correctly, I told you *no police work*."

"I didn't go looking for this. It fell in my lap."

"Make it quick. If I'm late, they'll both be on my case."

I filled him in on my conversation with Gale.

He must have sat down. I heard his chair scraping the floor. "This guy, Jerry Finnegan? He's up in Bellingham working on a construction site?"

"According to the girl."

"Shit. Margaret's going to kill me. Okay. I've got work to do on this. Don't go looking for trouble, but anything else you get, you call me right away. Got it?"

"Got it. How about a 'Thanks, Nate'?"

"Yeah. Thanks, Nate." He cut the connection.

The old woman was loading the bags of groceries into the back of an ancient Subaru Outback. An old man sitting behind the steering wheel and smoking a pipe yelled something at her. She yelled something back and threw a box of Tide into the back seat.

CHAPTER 28

An epiphany.

Rowdy had finished with the girl, now it was Bernie's turn. Christ almighty. This wasn't working out.

Aroused? Yeah. But his mind was definitely not on the task at hand. He couldn't get off.

Fake it? Well, that was something he'd never done before.

Rowdy wouldn't know the difference, and it sure as hell wouldn't matter to the girl. She'd be dead in a few minutes.

Then he thought about the joyful sound Chet's head made when it split open on the toilet bowl. His back went into spasms and he exploded with the most intense orgasm he'd ever felt. He had the sense he was going to die, right then and there. The girl lurched against the restraints as his dazed eyes watched the horror in hers.

Bernie collapsed – couldn't catch his breath. Wow, that was a first! Rolling over on the cold table, his bare back flinched on the frigid stainless steel. He arched and pulled up his pants. Rowdy was big on going at it buck naked. Bernie always preferred to just drop trousers.

He glanced at Rowdy, slumped in the folding chair taking a drag on a joint. Rowdy liked a good high after the first go.

"Give me a minute, Bernie. Got to get tuned up for round two."

Bernie had to get out of the basement. He needed a drink – bad. A cigarette even seemed like a good idea, and he hadn't smoked in years. "I'm going upstairs. You clean this mess up."

Rowdy's mouth hung open. "What? You're not going to finish the job? You always finish the job."

"Not tonight. You do it." Bernie slid off the table, his feet unsteady on the floor. He took a few shaky steps toward the stairs.

Rowdy got up from the chair; the joint between his fingers. "But, Bernie…"

"But Bernie, nothing. Just get it done."

"Now I don't feel like doing it again, if you don't want to." Rowdy took a long pull on the joint and looked up mournfully as Bernie mounted the stairs. He mumbled at Bernie's back, "And, I never clean up as good as you. What if I make a mistake?"

The door at the top of the stairs was jammed, again. Bernie kicked it open with his boot, yelling back down the stairs, "How many times do I have to tell you to fix this damn door." The evening was going from bad to worse.

Bernie walked down the hallway to the old musty smelling pantry. Rowdy didn't do shit to keep the place up. On the shelf he spied a bottle of cheap bourbon half full and resting next to a century-old box of Wheaties. His hand wrapped around the bottle. Something had made the bottle stick to the shelf. He broke it lose and brought it into the kitchen.

He looked around. "There better be a clean glass around here somewhere."

From the basement, he heard a thrashing noise, then silence. He stared at the bottle. For a second, he couldn't remember what it was or what it was doing in his hand.

A vision of Chet crumpled on the bathroom floor brought on a soothing sensation. Then he thought about shooting the transvestite. He actually began to feel better. Something was changing inside of him, something basic.

Bernie reached for a glass on the counter. His mind didn't register whether or not the glass was clean. He raised the bottle to his mouth. Gripping the cork with his teeth he twisted the bottle. The cork didn't want to come out. He jerked his head back without a single thought to how he might appear to his audience with missing teeth.

The cork popped out. He let it drop from his lips.

Two fingers was about what he needed. He poured four and tossed it down his throat. Man, was that some nasty tasting shit. More than likely left over from his grandpa's time.

The whiskey hit his stomach. The burn wasn't pleasant – not like good single malt scotch. No, not as pleasant, but it brought on an epiphany.

A big one.

No more snatching women. Fuck Rowdy and the farm. He was done with all of this shit – the women, their terror, the sex, the finishing up. He was moving on to better things. All he could see was Chet's head bouncing off the toilet bowl.

Sitting down, he poured four more fingers. Yep, time to move on. Leaning back in the old kitchen chair, Bernie thought about how to find his next man – and kill him.

CHAPTER 29

Wednesday evening

"It's open." Abby's voice came clear as a bell through her front door.

I turned the doorknob, looking in before I stepped across the threshold. Down the long entryway leading to her kitchen, I saw her leaning against a wall with a cellphone cradled between her shoulder and her ear.

Her house was in the West Hills. Not that far from my condo as the crow flies but over two miles by road.

I'd parked in the circular drive that arched through the massive front yard. The house was new. At first glance, it appeared to be stone. Her ex-husband must have a good job.

The thought passed through my mind, *what does she see in me?*

I stepped into the red-tiled entryway. To my right down three steps was a large room with an off-white carpet and matching leather furniture. A large glassed-in fireplace surrounded by black stone covered most of the far wall. There may have been more square feet in the living room than in my entire condo.

She turned towards me and waved her free hand. She pointed a finger in the air, which I assume meant, "Give me a minute."

I closed the door and wandered down the hallway. Twenty-five feet down and to the left was an office filled with modern leather furnishings. A steel table supported two of the largest monitors I'd ever seen.

"You're early." She came up behind me. I felt her hand rest against my back.

I turned around and slid my hands around her waist, gently pulling her toward me. I closed my eyes and brought my lips towards hers. I felt her head swivel, just the slightest. My lips brushed her right cheek. My nose made an uncalculated collision with her ear.

Uh-oh.

I regained my composure and released her.

Her hands went to her waist and slid on down her hips, like she was brushing something off.

Double Uh-oh.

"How are you?" I couldn't think of anything stupider to say.

I could have said, "You look lovely" because she did. Very lovely, in fact. But, I didn't.

She turned and walked toward the kitchen. I obediently followed her.

The plan was to go to a fundraiser for the new children's cancer center. Everybody who is anybody would be there. Thanks to Abby, that group would include me tonight.

She walked across the checkerboard tile, turned, and leaned against the refrigerator. There were photographs of small children stuck to the doors. Nephews and nieces? Maybe she would tell me.

"We need a little talk, before we go out tonight."

Guess the introduction to the nephews and nieces would come later, if at all.

"Sure." That's me, one-hundred percent cooperation.

She crossed her arms over her chest. The slightest hint of pink was spreading along her beautiful cheekbones. Was that a miniscule tightening of the jaw – getting ready for my lie – which would be my natural response to the question she was about to ask?

And her question was, "There's a small restaurant out on Cesar Chavez. Very upscale. Juju's Joint. Do you know it?"

I could get through this. No lies. "Yes."

She said, "The lady, the owner, Julie…."

"Yes. I know her. We had a short relationship a while back."

Some of the tension went out of her shoulders. "Just before the hospital, where we met? Before you were shot by that old woman?"

"Yes. Things didn't work out between Julie and me. I…"

"That isn't really my question."

I looked at her.

She said, "Julie's on the board of the cancer center."

"Okay, it'll be nice to see her again. Nice lady. She…"

Her shoulders were getting tense again. "I spoke with her at the board meeting a couple of days ago. Funny how one thing leads to another?"

I shrugged. "Yeah. I know."

Here it comes.

"She mentioned a woman she'd met. Well, not really met, the woman spoke to her briefly at a wedding you two attended."

"Our mutual friends got married on the coast."

She glanced around the room, like she was trying to find something. "This woman was an artist. Is an artist, I guess? Lives in New York?"

"Yes. We…"

"She has a restraining order against you."

Do not blow this. "Yes."

She placed a hand on her forehead. "I need to understand this."

I said, "Yes, you do."

She met my eyes. "So?" Then she looked away, but I saw the tears welling up.

I said, "It's not an easy thing for me to talk about. It may take a while."

The tears were making tiny lines down her cheeks.

I swallowed. "We may have to blow off the fundraiser."

She shook her head. "Shit! I can't blow off the goddamn fundraiser. Shit!"

When I stepped toward her, her hand pressed firmly against my chest. "No. Please. Not now." The hands went back to her waist and she made the same motion, brushing them down her hips. "I need to clean up. Give me a few minutes."

"Okay." I stepped back.

She started down the hallway and waved a hand at the fridge. "There's beer and white wine in there. Help yourself."

She disappeared around the corner.

I turned to the fridge, started to open it, and saw the photographs again. I dropped my hand. I could wait for a beer.

CHAPTER 30

Wednesday night

That night, I had my picture taken seven times. Twice with Abby and five times with various groups of well-heeled Portlanders. The standard pose was to lean into the group or the person you were with, raise your flute, and smile. After the second snapshot, I had the procedure down pat. I couldn't wait for the next issue of *Portland Monthly*.

Despite our earlier conversation, or the lack of it, Abby was unusually affectionate. She'd hold my hand when talking to other people and give me the stray kiss as we mingled.

About an hour into the event, I looked up to see Art and Margaret across the room and deep in conversation with one of the doctors. I felt relief just seeing them. Margaret was stunning. Art looked like a cop.

I was getting antsy for the announcement telling the crowd dinner was served when Abby gave my sleeve a little tug.

As I turned, a couple joined us. Abby said, "Bernie and Missy, this is my friend Nate. He's new to the foundation."

I'd seen the couple before.

They had the same look on their faces I must have had on mine.

Missy kind of sputtered. "I think we've met."

I nodded. "I believe so."

With a big smile on his face, Bernie stuck his hand out. "You're the guy who duck-walked Chet out the restaurant."

Not too gently, Missy patted his arm. "Bernie, that's not nice. Poor Chet."

The lightbulb in my head went on. "Oh, you're the news anchor and weatherman."

Missy nodded in the affirmative and Bernie beamed.

"Chet was our sports anchor. He had a horrible accident that night." Missy looked about to cry.

"Drunk as a skunk, fell in the crapper, split his head open on the toilet bowl." The tragedy didn't seem to bother Bernie as much as it did Missy.

Missy was getting upset. "Bernie, please!"

Bernie's smile became a little less luminous. "Right, Missy. That was thoughtless. Sorry."

A waiter in a tuxedo came strutting through the ballroom ringing a chime and announcing, "Dinner is served."

That message broke the tension in our little group.

We all shook hands and agreed it was great to meet each other.

As Bernie and Missy turned to find their table, Bernie put his hand beside his mouth, gave me a conspiring wink, and whispered, "The guy was an asshole."

Missy took his arm and they were off.

No matter how fancy the venue – chicken is chicken. Do with it what you want. It's hard to call it anything else. I ate mine, drank some wine, and agreed with the other couples at our table that the meal was fabulous. Donnie would've looked at me and shaken his head in shame. Bless his heart.

After the molten lava chocolate cake had been served, and devoured, Art made his way over to our table. I saw him coming, excused myself, and stood up. Abby was deep in discussion with a stately woman whose name was on the ballet theater a block down the street.

"Think there's a bottle of good scotch around here?" Art could only handle so much bubbly.

I spied a small bar in the corner. "Let's give that a try." I pointed in the direction and we took off.

Once armed with two glasses of Glenlivet, we studied the crowd.

I took a sip. "See any bad guys?"

"There's a loudmouth at our table I'm tempted to take down to the station, just to shut him up."

"Lucky you."

Art swirled the ice in his glass. "Margaret's been asked to be on the board. The Commissioner thinks that's a great idea."

"He didn't ask for your opinion?"

Art looked at me. "Don't be a dumbass." His glass stopped half way to his mouth. He was looking over my shoulder. "Oh, no. Here comes the loudmouth now."

I turned in time to take the brunt of Bernie tripping into me. Champagne splashed onto my suit. He didn't seem to notice.

He wiped his nose on the sleeve of his tailored jacket. "Well, great to see two members of the law enforcement community keeping an eye out." A dribble or two was left in his flute. He threw his head back and downed it. Bernie was going to need a ride home.

I took a half step back. "Sorry Bernie, but I don't really qualify."

"You're not a cop?" Bernie pointed a finger somewhere in Art's direction. "Well, he's a cop. His wife told me he's a cop, a colonel or something." He brought the flute up again, somewhat mystified to find it empty.

Art turned to me, and like we'd just met, shook my hand, and said, "Nice to meet you." He waved a couple of fingers at Bernie, "See you" and beat a coward's retreat.

Bernie grabbed me by the arm, pulling me toward the bar. I looked at Art's back moving at almost a trot toward Margaret. He's saved my life more than once, and I knew I owed him, but this bordered on the unforgivable.

"I would have sworn you were a cop." Then to the bartender, "More of the same for my friend." Back to me, "What's your poison?"

"Diet Coke."

That cracked him up. Bernie pointed at me and told the bartender, "Best bourbon you got."

The bartender looked at me. I shook my head. Bernie was distracted, watching a twenty-something in a short dress with no back slink by. The bartender filled the glass from the soft drink hose. "Bourbon it is" and handed it to me.

Bernie looked down into his empty flute, annoyed it was still empty. "Champagne!" he barked, as if it was the bartender's fault.

The poor guy opened a new bottle and filled Bernie's flute. Bernie beamed, pleased with the outcome.

Before the bartender could stick the fresh bottle of Moet Extra Brut up his ass, I spun Bernie around and led him to the center of the room.

"You're not a cop? You sure as hell look like a cop, act like a cop." He put his head next to my suitcoat and took a sniff. "Smell like a cop, too."

I seriously considered going back for the bottle of Moet and the bartender.

"What'a you do?" He downed the flute in one gulp.

"Insurance fraud investigation. Nothing exciting. Nothing like being a TV star."

Here came Missy, looking sober. Thank God.

"Bernie, give me your keys." She looked at me and rolled her eyes. "Never saw him do this before." She turned back to Bernie. "I always thought you could hold your booze." She shook her head and walked him toward the exit.

As I gave them a little goodbye wave, I heard her say, "Who was that guy?"

Bernie stopped and turned back to me. "Just what I'm looking for."

CHAPTER 31

Thursday morning

When we returned to Abby's house, our conversation continued – just not in the way I expected. We made love the instant we stepped through the doorway. A short while later in her bed, I talked – or explained – or something. Abby cried. We made love again. We talked. Abby cried, and then I held her while we fell asleep.

A little before noon, I kissed her at the front door. We held each other for a long time and then I got in the pickup. From the shadowed doorway, she watched me pull out of the circular drive.

Did we solve anything or come to an understanding? I wasn't sure. I wasn't sure if she was sure. These relationship things aren't simple, and I'm not the poster boy for successful relationships.

I'd told her the truth – my truth. Molly's truth would've been completely different but still the truth. Like I said, relationships aren't simple.

We'd agreed to go on seeing each other. Abby made that clear, and it was what I wanted, too.

I stopped for a red light at the junction of Miller and Barnes Road and noticed the man-made waterfall across the intersection was foaming.

I said to the windshield, "I wonder why it does that?"

Donnie reached over and switched off the radio. "What? Foam like that?"

"Yeah."

He looked straight ahead, as confused as I was. He said, "Beats the shit out of me." Then he turned and faced me full on. The cancer had done a real job on him. He was gaunt. The skin on his hands a pale gray, his cheeks sunken, and his thin white hair almost a memory. His voice was hoarse. "You gonna mess this gal up, too?"

CHAPTER 32

Friday morning

As I sat in my office sipping the day's first cup of coffee, Leo called trying to reach Orlando. He was frustrated Orlando wasn't answering his cell, and I was tempted to tell him Orlando had caller ID. Leo didn't want to talk to me, which meant he had a "special needs" case. Orlando handles the "special needs" side of our business.

I told him Orlando and his pals were probably down in the Willamette Valley doing a hands-on audit of the grape harvest. If the vintner wasn't sweating bullets with all of this help, I'd be surprised.

Leo didn't appear overjoyed that Orlando was taking a little time off. I promised I'd get in touch with my business partner and reassured him that any Lumberjack Mutual need was our need. He mumbled something and hung up.

Just as I put the office phone down, my cell rang showing Art's number. I didn't bother with the niceties. "Thanks for bailing and leaving me with the drunk."

"You're welcome. Anything for a buddy. However, that isn't why I called."

"And?"

"Not that it's any of your business, but you did give me the tip on Finnegan."

"You found him?" I sat up straight and grabbed a pencil.

"Not exactly."

"Huh?"

He asked, "You ever hear of Maple Falls? It's east of Bellingham on Mt. Baker Highway."

"No." I didn't know every backwoods burg in Washington.

"Finnegan was pouring concrete on a job for the State Parks and Recreation department. The local sheriff's office sent two deputies out to talk to him. They charged in with lights flashing. The foreman told them Finnegan was working on site, but when they went to find him, he was long gone. A crane-operator reported seeing someone *run like hell* into the woods about the same time the cruiser pulled in."

I put my pencil down. "If it was Finnegan, sounds like you've got a solid suspect."

"We're sure it was him running through the trees. By the time the deputies located his motel room Finnegan had been there and hightailed it. His stuff was gone and so was his vehicle. You'd think the sheriff would've nabbed him by now, but no such luck."

"Do the State Police have his mother's trailer staked out in Forest Grove?"

"Yeah. There and two other spots he might show up." Art paused. "Ready for the icing on the cake?"

"Fire away."

"He was a fill-in on the concrete crew at the Sweet Mackerel for two days after Cliffy's girlfriend disappeared. The construction superintendent said Finnegan wasn't the brightest bulb in the crew. Said he was glad to see him gone. Finnegan spent most of his working hours spouting off bible verses and pestering the crew to pray with him."

"Art, is Cliffy off your radar?"

He let out a long breath. "As much as I love the thought of Cliffy off the streets and preferably behind bars, Cliffy is not the fucking problem here."

"Does Cliffy know about Finnegan?"

"No, not yet. I was planning to give Ruth that task."

"Mind if I tag along with her? Cliffy's in a bad state."

"Nothing Ruth can't handle, but I'll ask her to call you." Art was done filling me in. The line went dead.

CHAPTER 33

The car looked like somebody rolled it.

It was dark and raining hard. Bernie was a quarter mile from the farm when he drove past the vehicle. The big Mercedes G Class was in the weeds several yards off the gravel road. He'd almost missed it; his mind being on the police captain and the investigator.

He was ready to flip a coin over the two men. Would it be the rude cop, or the insurance investigator? It would be a hard decision, but he was leaning toward the investigator. A cop would just be too high a risk. But killing a cop, now that made his dick hard. Nope. It was early days with killing men, best not to be an overachiever.

He felt like a new man. Now, he needed to get Rowdy onboard. A thought was forming in his head about removing Rowdy from the board when he noticed a reflection off the side of the road. It made him hit the brakes and back up.

There was a big-ass SUV thirty feet to his left in the high weeds. Someone had wedged it in next to a tall blueberry bush. Two kids fucking? Not in that car. It was a Mercedes – one of those things James Bond would drive in the jungle or out in the desert. Maybe it was a bank president letting the new cashier go down on him?

Bernie pulled over and shut off the engine. He took a small flashlight from the glovebox and got out of the car. It *wasn't raining quite as hard now, but he wasn't really dressed for wading through the weeds and mud. Screw it. Something wasn't right. He stepped into the weeds and felt his new Italian moccasins slip on the mud.*

Shit.

Slowly, he worked his way to the passenger door; a river of mud was trying to suck his shoes off with every step. The car looked as if someone had rolled it. The driver's side was covered with mud and sod stuck out from the molding. Sod? There wasn't any sod around here. What the hell was going on? He peered inside but couldn't see shit. He turned the flashlight on and pointed it into the vehicle, fully expecting to see two startled faces glare back at him. It was empty.

Now Bernie knew. Something was absolutely not right. Shit.

He shined the light down on the weeds. Someone had walked away from the vehicle, mashing down the weeds, and was headed toward the farmhouse.

Fuck.

He sloshed back to his car; his moccasins came off twice before he got to the road. He paused with his hand on the door handle realizing whoever it was, they'd hear him drive up. It could be more than one guy.

Shit, Shit, Shit.

Did his car have a jack? He'd never looked. He popped the trunk and pulled up the carpet.

Yes. Reaching in the wheel well he felt the jack. Now, did it have a handle? He ripped off the plastic wrapper. Bingo, a jack handle, just like in the old cars. Thank fucking God.

Bernie made a mental note to buy a gun when he got back to town.

He shut the trunk, turned off the flashlight, hefted the jack handle, and began the trek up the road to the farmhouse. Despite everything, a frantic giggle shot out between his lips. Just as he'd predicted on the six o'clock news, the rain was picking up.

The driveway to the house snaked through dense brush. He couldn't see the lights on the front porch until he was right on it.

It was dead quiet. Bernie crept across the flower beds his grandma had planted when he and Rowdy were little. He thought of the dead animals they'd buried there. The young girl, the first girl, was buried there too. She was a lot deeper down than the animals. When they buried her, it seemed like they'd dug almost to China. For weeks afterward, he'd been scared shitless, waking in the middle of the night, sure the girl's hand was reaching up through the topsoil. Rowdy likened it to The Night of the Living Dead or one of those other zombie movies.

He stepped up on the low stone wall that went around the house and peeked in the kitchen window. The lights were on. He could see into the kitchen and down the long hallway to the parlor. The door to the basement was wide open. Rowdy must be down there.

Bernie stepped down from the wall and looked over at the open garage. He could see Rowdy's van inside. He moved away from the house toward the garage and slipped in through the side door. He put his hand on the hood of the van. It was still warm.

Had Rowdy gone out for a girl and not told him? The dumb son of a bitch better not have. Maybe he'd gone out for beer or groceries. Shit. It was way too late to be out shopping. Bernie knew it was a girl – had to be. *The dumbfuck.*

The kitchen door flew open banging against a rocking chair.

Bernie spun around.

He watched a bare-assed naked girl jump off the steps and run down the dark drive.

As she raced toward the gravel road, her gut-wrenching screams ripped through the falling rain. "Pomogi mne! Pomogi mne! Pomogi mne!"

It didn't sound like Spanish and sure as hell wasn't English.

He heard another scream. This one wasn't in any language. It was just a scream, and it came from the house.

Bernie ran out the side door of the garage with the jack handle raised high.

The kitchen door hung open. The top hinge had broken off. Bernie kicked off the muddy moccasins and stepped through the doorway. He heard another scream from the basement followed by a loud slap and a voice shouting, "Shut the fuck up!"

Heavy steps were coming up the basement stairs – too heavy to be Rowdy's.

Shit.

Bernie jumped into a narrow space between the refrigerator and the cabinets.

A big guy with a head full of blond hair passed in front of him. The guy was built like one of those wrestlers on late night TV.

Bernie took a step out, wound up, and smashed the jack handle into the blond hairdo. The guy wobbled forward, spun around, and dropped to his knees. He looked up at Bernie through stark white eyeballs.

Bernie did another wind up. The makeshift weapon came crashing down. Blood flew everywhere. The guy was still on his knees with his head wobbling.

Blood flowed down his face, over his jacket, and onto the kitchen floor. Bernie put his right foot on the muscular chest and gave it a push. The body flopped over; its left leg was jerking. Then it went still.

Bernie stood over the man; the jack handle ready. The body laid there for a few seconds, and then a stream of air leaked through its lips. The wide-open eyes stared at the kitchen ceiling.

He brought the weapon down once more. This time it was just sloppy. No more blood. No jerking legs. No whoosh of air. Only a mushy thud.

Bernie heard something moving around in the basement.

A large pistol was tucked into the dead man's belt. Bernie pulled it out, gawking at it. All Bernie knew was that he had a gun in his hand. The thing was heavy and chrome with nice wood on the handle.

He pointed the barrel toward the cellar stairs and yelled, "Rowdy!"

A thrashing noise arose from the basement.

Bernie kept the gun pointed in front of him and started down the stairs.

Three-quarters of the way down he saw Rowdy sprawled on the floor. His wrists were tied to the steel leg of the table, and a rag jammed in his mouth.

Bernie rushed to his cousin and knelt next to him. Rowdy's face was smashed to a pulp. The dead guy upstairs had worked him over pretty well.

Rowdy's eyes bulged from their sockets.

Bernie stood up, opened a drawer in the table, and took out a box cutter. He got back down on his knees and began sawing the duct tape wrapped around his cousin's wrist.

For a second, he stopped sawing and thought about plunging the blade into Rowdy's throat.

Bernie gripped the box cutter tighter and sawed through the tape.

He jerked the rag out of Rowdy's mouth.

Rowdy rolled around on the basement floor sobbing and blubbering, "Bernie! He was gonna kill me. Jesus. Bernie, Bernie, he was gonna kill me." Rowdy's whole body trembled.

Bernie climbed back up the stairs to the kitchen. He returned with the remainder of the whiskey from the other night and handed the bottle to Rowdy.

Rowdy tipped it and gulped down most of what was left. He set the bottle between his legs. Then he gagged as if he was going to vomit. Bernie jumped back.

Rowdy caught his breath and took another swig. "I was tying the girl down when this big fucker comes down the stairs with a fuckin' gun." Rowdy wiped a hand across his mouth and brought the bottle back to his lips.

The whiskey dripped down his chin. "He hit me. Hit me in the face with the gun. Then he must've tied me up." Rowdy held his head. "When I come round he was talking to the girl in some fucked-up foreign language. He cut her loose and slapped her around. She took off up the stairs. He rooted around the basement for a minute, and then he went upstairs."

"Yeah." Bernie nodded his head.

"Jesus, Bernie. Is he upstairs?"

"I killed him."

Rowdy looked up the stairs. "Is the girl there too?"

The girl? "Shit!"

Bernie took the stairs three at a time.

He ran outside onto the small porch. The girl could be a mile down the road by now.

He slipped back into his muddy moccasins, shoved the gun down into the waistband of his pants, and ran down the drive. The rain was colder and coming in sheets.

Ten minutes later, almost like a miracle, the clouds parted, and he caught a flash of bare white skin in the moonlight. The girl leapt from the side of the road into the tall weeds. Bernie ran to where she'd gone off the road – near where the Mercedes was parked. He switched on the flashlight and walked into the weeds. "Hello! Is there someone out here?"

The girl raised her head. "Pomogi mne. Help me!"

"What happened here?"

The girl's voice was shaking. "Help me mister. Please help me." She had to be freezing.

"I have a blanket in my car. I'll get it." Bernie jogged over to his car.

He started the engine and turned on the headlights. Then, he walked back with the blanket and tossed it to her.

She wrapped the blanket around her thin frame and staggered out of the weeds.

Bernie pointed to his car. "Let me get you to a hospital."

"Oh, mister. I'm so scared." The girl stepped in front of him while shuffling toward the headlights.

Bernie took the chrome pistol from his pants, pointed it at the back of her head, and squeezed the trigger.

CHAPTER 34

Saturday morning

Cliffy did not take the news well.

I felt bad for him. Ruth was professional, and I think helpful. But I knew she didn't really give a shit. Like several Portland Police officers, she shared a history with Cliffy. She'd not reaped the benefit of knowing the new and improved model.

"When do you think you'll have this guy Finnegan in custody?" Cliffy was pulling up a red and yellow argyle sock. It was nice to see it matched his other sock. His wardrobe for the weekend was a pair of black jeans and a green Timbers tee-shirt. It could have been a whole lot worse.

Ruth was keeping her distance, trying hard not to take on a defensive posture. "It won't be long. We're not chasing a Rhodes Scholar here."

Cliffy gave her a skeptical look, stood up, and walked in his stocking feet to the kitchen. Looking back over his shoulder, he said, "Would either of you care for some coffee?"

Ruth gave an involuntary shudder.

I told him, "No, thanks."

"You sure, Nate?" He looked disappointed.

"Yeah. I'm sure. But thanks anyway."

He picked up a jar of Nescafé. I think the responsible thing for me to have done would have been to slap it out of his hand, but he needed a little self-abuse.

Shakely, he reached for a mug. "I hope you find him soon. If I find him first, I'm going to kill him."

"Jesus, Cliffy! Will you not do this?" I looked over at Ruth.

She'd crossed her arms over her chest. I imagined she wanted to drag him kicking and screaming down to the cruiser.

"I don't care if she hears me or not."

Ruth said to me, "Can you keep this loose cannon under control?"

"Don't know. I can try."

"Any other questions, Cliffy?" Without waiting for an answer, she stepped toward the door. "We'll keep you informed of our progress."

Her hand on the knob, she turned back to him. "You get anymore crazy thoughts in your head; you just keep them there. Understand?"

Cliffy was leaning over the sink – head down and his back to her. "Yes, officer."

Ruth gave me a last look and walked out.

This was my first visit to Cliffy's new abode. He and Felicienne had moved in together to this penthouse condo in the north end of the Pearl District. The place was neat and clean, nice furnishings, with only the slightest hint of a dirty towel, a stray sock, or underwear scattered about.

Orlando and I'd once shared the unfortunate experience of visiting Cliffy's bachelor pad in Northeast, off 82nd Avenue. That had been several years ago, but some memories won't ever fade away.

He spooned the Nescafé into a cup of boiling water and returned to the living room. "I was sure Karolek did it."

I sat down on a wood bench. "Why would he want her dead? She was going to make him some money. The new club."

"She talked back. Argued with him. Karolek doesn't like that, especially from a woman."

Cliffy's cell rang. He picked it up. There was a puzzled look on his face as he stared at the number displayed on the screen.

He'd started to put it in his pocket when I said, "Go ahead and take it. It might be important."

Cliffy brought the phone to his ear. "Hello."

He looked genuinely surprised. "Yeah?"

Cliffy began nodding his head in approval of whatever was being said.

He looked up at me and spoke into the phone. "He's here. Yeah, standing in my living room." He made a couple of more nods. "Yeah, sure."

He handed me the phone.

Before I could say hello, I heard, "Harver?" The voice was raspy.

"Yes."

"Thought of something, after we talked."

"Who is this?"

"Who the fuck you think it is? Jesus. It's Mickey."

"O'Reilly?"

"Who'd you expect? Alex Trebeck? You done askin' questions?"

"Yeah, Mick. What do you need?"

"Me? I don't need anything. Maybe a hard-on once before I die. It's you that needs something."

"What is it I need, Mick?" I looked over at Cliffy. He mouthed "The Razor."

I nodded.

"Remember that problem I handled back in '98?"

"Our discussion over lunch at John Day's?" I was amazed he still remembered it.

"You betcha."

"Go ahead."

"Well, maybe I didn't exactly finish the job."

"Hefty said you took out both guys. Two brothers."

He sputtered, "Not over the damn phone. You're as bad as Hefty was."

"Was?"

The other end of the phone went silent for a few seconds. When he came back, all of the bluster had gone out of his voice. "Yeah. Hefty's in Regency. Stroke. A bad one."

"A stroke? He's not doing well?" I glanced at Cliffy again.

"Well, this morning he was drooling out the right side of his mouth. I gotta say, that's a step up from the way he looked yesterday."

"Sorry, Mick."

"Fuck it. Nobody's gonna live forever. Could be me layin' there soaking the pillow."

"Like I said. I'm sorry, Mick. What is it I need to know?"

"There was a couple of kids on the farm, where I… uh, you know."

"Keep going."

"Well… uh, actually, one of the brothers was dead when I got there and …"

"You sure you want to talk over the phone?"

I heard the snap of a lighter and a long exhale. "What the hell. They gonna throw me in jail? Place to sleep, three meals a day, decent medical care, lots of friends to talk to. Hells bells, I'll be dead by the time I come to trial."

Hard to argue with him.

"I was tellin' Cliffy about our conversation, when he said you were there." I heard him inhale a few cubic meters of cigarette smoke. "What are you doing hanging out with Cliffy. I gave you more credit."

"Long story, Mick."

"I want to take you guys somewhere, 'cept it's you gotta take me. Can't drive at night no more. Hell, can't drive when the sun's out. I'm pretty much fucked if I can't walk somewhere."

I felt myself slipping down the rabbit hole to Wonderland. "Mick, is this important? I've got stuff on my plate."

"Fuck your plate. Get Cliffy and get over here." He hung up.

I looked at Cliffy. "What the hell was that about? He wants us to pick him up and go somewhere."

Cliffy shrugged, but I caught a strange gleam in his eyes.

CHAPTER 35

Saturday afternoon

We drove into town and found a place to park a block from my office. The more I thought about Mick O'Reilly, the more I convinced myself that if I wasn't armed, we might end up being very sorry. A snub-nosed .38 seemed like a good choice. After I got out of the pickup, I turned back to Cliffy. "Why don't you stay here. Protect the car. Never can tell when one of your underage gangsters might try to rip me off."

"None of my apprentices have authorization to operate in this area." He took his phone out. "I've got calls to make."

I bought forty-five minutes of parking time and jogged up 3rd Avenue.

THE DOOR TO THE OFFICE WAS PARTIALLY OPEN.

I slipped in quietly to find Orlando and his pal Torres studying the screen of Orlando's laptop. Instinctively, Torres slid his hand into his jacket. I doubt he even realized he did it.

His hand emerged empty when he recognized me. A warm smile filled his still handsome face. "Nate, my man."

"Torres, don't tell me you went in on this vineyard with Orlando."

"Thought it'd look good with me on the cover of *Wine Spectator*. Middle-aged aristocratic Spaniard strolling through the vines. Morning mist filling the valley."

"Yeah, either *Wine Spectator* or *Soldier of Fortune*. Dream on." I spun the dial on my gun safe. "Spaniard? Thought you were third generation Mexican out of the LA barrios?"

"Catalan blood line." He plucked a Churchill from his shirt pocket, stuck it between his teeth, and focused on an item Orlando was pointing to on the screen.

I snapped the holstered .38 onto the back of my belt, shut the safe door, and made the mistake of glancing at Orlando's computer screen. Nobody had to tell me I was looking at a map of Syria. "No. Fuck me. You're not really thinking about this?"

Orlando didn't even bother to look up from the screen. "Money to be made."

Torres began scribbling in a notebook he held in his hand. "Best opportunity to come down the pike in quite a while."

I watched as Orlando marked a route through Iraq into Dayr Az Zawr. "You guys are fucking nuts."

Torres looked up from his scribbling, giving the cigar a Groucho jiggle. "Want to come along?"

Orlando glanced up at me. "You getting any closer to finding us some office help? I may need some clerical support soon."

"On it." I lied. Just trying to imagine what these two were planning made my heart pound. "I gotta go. Cliffy's waiting down in the truck."

As I stepped out the door, Orlando's voice followed me. "And you call us crazy?"

When I got back to the truck, I found Cliffy deep in conversation with one of the homeless Native Americans who frequent the area. Before waving him away, Cliffy slipped him what looked like a twenty.

I climbed in behind the wheel. "What was that about?"

"Chief Swift Eagle always has a tidbit of useful information. Tell Art to cultivate the original Americans more often. He might learn a thing or two."

"Chief Swift Eagle? You're shitting me. Thought his name was Wally."

Cliffy countered, "I prefer to use his title when I address him. I believe he prefers it as well."

I cranked the engine and rolled my eyes. It's hazardous to one's mental health to spend too much time around Cliffy, and our day was only starting.

Traffic was backed up at the turn from 3rd Avenue onto Alder. Two old men pushing their oxygen tubes in strollers were taking their time crossing the street. An image of Hefty whisked through my mind. We sat through two lights before finally making the turn. I gunned it up the ramp onto the Morrison Bridge and moved into the right lane once we got on Belmont.

Cliffy directed me through Southeast Portland to Mick's place. The Craftsman house was a few blocks south of Division on 33rd Avenue. Mick was within walking distance of all the flashy bars and restaurants. But, imagining him mingling with a crowd of twenty-something girls and hipster guys was a real stretch.

Mick's house was the nicest on the block with its fresh paint and a manicured terraced front lawn. There was even a swing and two Adirondack chairs on the big porch. It made me wonder if any dead bodies were fertilizing the lovely rose bushes.

I parked in the drive. We got out and started up the walk when the front door opened and out stepped Mick. He was dressed to the nines in corduroy pants, a suede hunting jacket, Wellington boots, and a deer stalker cap. I would have laughed if not for the AR-15 assault rifle he cradled in his arms.

I stuck the palm of my hand out. "Whoa, Mick. Why the big gun?"

Mick barked, "I go out, I go out strapped."

Cliffy didn't seem bothered in the least.

Mick snuggled the rifle to his chest, looked down, and stepped off the porch onto the concrete stairs leading to his front walk. Cliffy bounded up the steps and took Mick's elbow.

"I got you Mick." Cliffy helped him down the remaining steps.

Once they were safely on the walk, he jerked his elbow from Cliffy's grip. Mick glared at me with a scowl on his face. "It ain't that I need help. Just can't see shit through these trifocals. Take my life in my hands every time I head down a set of stairs."

I pointed over to my pickup. "Well, Mick, it'll be a little tight in the truck. Cliffy's gonna have to ride in the back seat." I might've felt a twinge of guilt. The Japanese engineer who designed the rear seat had not thought a human being would actually ride there.

As we stood there, a horn blared followed immediately by the screech of brakes. A rant of obscenities echoed up the quiet street. Then an engine roared. From the left a bright yellow Range Rover sped up the street. The driver hit the brakes, causing the SUV to swerve towards the curb in front of Mick's house. The vehicle bounced up on the sidewalk shuddering to a stop.

Cliffy raced down the walk shouting at the driver, "What took you so long?"

The driver scampered around the bright yellow hood. "We came as soon as you called. The Hawthorne Bridge was up."

I recognized the driver as a member of Cliffy's teenage entourage. He looked a tad older than I remembered from a previous encounter on Alberta Street. He still hadn't solved his acne issues, and I doubted he was old enough to drive. Cliffy threw his arm around the boy's skinny shoulders and squeezed him like a proud father.

I could make out another figure sitting silently in the back seat, apparently waiting for the reunion to wind down. Cliffy didn't appear to be paying any attention to this guy. If it was a guy. Hard to tell.

Cliffy marched his protégée cum driver up the walk. "Mick, you ride with the Nateman. Lead the way. We'll be right behind you."

I looked at the Range Rover, top of the line, over $100,000. Where on Earth could Cliffy get that kind of cash? Maybe there is money in the bottom of the criminal barrel after all.

Cliffy climbed in the passenger's side of the yellow SUV. He glanced at the rider in the back seat. I thought I saw Cliffy flitch, but I might have imagined it.

I started towards the Tacoma. "Okay, Mick. It's you and me. You're the copilot."

"Hold up, youngster." Mick held his elbow out for me to take. "Help me to the car and don't say a fuckin' word."

I guided him to my truck. Christ – a half blind killer, two teen gangbangers, and Cliffy. Fuck. What was I getting into?

CHAPTER 36

Saturday afternoon

"Now Mick. Tell me again – where're we going and why are we going there?" I gripped the steering wheel with both hands. The Tacoma bounced in and out of deep potholes in the gravel lane. It was the third backwoods road we'd been down in the last hour. Each one was rougher than the one before. The one thing they bore in common was a view of Mount Hood. I knew we were well past Sandy, but I'd long since lost track of exactly where.

Mick shaded his eyes with his hand and glared out the windshield. "Fuck. This don't look right. Why can't you find the right damn road?"

"For Pete's sake, Mick. Remember, you're the navigator. This is your idea."

"If you could follow directions, it'd sure as hell help. Didn't I tell you to turn right a mile or so back?"

"Not that I recall. Listen, I'll pull over at the top of this rise and pray for cellphone reception. Maybe I can see where we are on Maps."

"What's Maps?"

"Never mind." I reached the crest of the hill and stopped at the edge of a cabbage field.

"Are those fuckin' cabbages?" Mick had his head out the window staring at the field. "Don't remember no cabbages when I was here last."

"When was that? Over twenty years ago?" Holding my phone in the air, I got out of the cab. Nope, no reception.

"Yeah, at least that. Those two kids must be grown up by now. Nasty little shits they were. Look at their dads. Pair of brothers. Liked to tie folks up and torture them, especially women. Still makes my skin crawl." With groans and a fair amount of swearing, he climbed down from the passenger's side.

I heard a hard spray of water hit the gravel on the road, but I didn't bother to turn around and look.

The sound trickled away. Mick let out a long sigh. "God, that felt good. If I can't bleed the lizard every fifteen minutes, it starts to burn."

It occurred to me that getting old might not be such a good idea.

The Range Rover bounded up the hill behind us and came to a stop on the opposite side of the road. Cliffy climbed out and looked around. "Where are we?" He stepped across the road right through the puddle Mick had just provided.

Mick was struggling to zip up his fly. "Watch where you're walkin', you dumb shit."

Cliffy looked down. "Christ, Mick. Did you just piss?" He stepped into the grass and rubbed the soles of his shoes on the tall shoots. "This is gross."

I couldn't recall what the plans for my day were when I woke up that morning. But, I was positive the events of the past few hours hadn't been a part of them.

I reached into the Tacoma's glove box where I'd stashed a pair of Zen Ray binoculars six months ago. I dug them out, adjusted the focus, and scanned the horizon. We were on a high point and the day was crystal clear. I'm not sure how far I could see, but it was miles.

There was a good-sized pond between where we were parked and Mount Hood. Not quite a lake but quite large. I spotted activity along the edge of the water. Two men stood by a large flatbed truck with a cable extending out into the pond. The other end of the cable was attached to something big and partially submerged in the water. It appeared the men were attempting to winch a vehicle out of the pond.

I offered the binoculars to Mick. "Take a gander, Mick. See if anything looks familiar."

He took off his trifocals, carefully folded them into a case, and put them in his jacket pocket. He held the binoculars to his eyes and fiddled with the focus. After a minute or so he bent over the Tacoma, rested his elbows on the hood and pointed at the pond. "What are those two dickheads doing out here?"

Cliffy and I looked at each other. Cliffy took the initiative. "What two dickheads?"

"Karolek and that fuckin' giant he keeps around for protection. Did you ever see two more worthless pieces of shit than those two?"

I was dumbfounded. "Mick, how can you tell it's Karolek? Those guys are over a mile away."

Mick turned his head and spat on the gravel. "My dick might not work, but there ain't nothing wrong with my eyes that these binoculars can't fix." He handed them back to me.

I focused on the pond. I had to admit, one of the figures was quite a bit larger than the other. Was it Karolek and Romeo? Hell, I had no clue.

The truck with the winch jerked back. The thing on the end cable was eased out of the water and drug onto the bank. It looked like a really big SUV. A Mercedes? Karolek drove a big-ass Mercedes. Thanks to a couple of bullets from Orlando into its tires, the last time I'd seen the vehicle it was laid out on its side in the cemetery.

Just when I was sure the day couldn't get any stranger. What the hell was going on?

We piled into our respective vehicles. I drove west for three-quarters of a mile and turned right down another dirt road that seemed to be headed in the general direction of the pond.

Mick reached into his jacket and came out with a flask. Unscrewing the top, he raised the silver container to his blue lips. He managed to get a good deal of the booze down the front of his jacket, but most of it hit his mouth. He handed the flask over to me. "Here. Have a swig. Good for what ails you."

"No thanks, Mick. I'm driving."

He gave me a funny look. "Never stopped me." He took another good jolt. This one was better aimed. Very little splashed on his jacket.

Mick had his head hanging out the side window. "You see those crazy fuckin' Russians yet?"

"Not yet. But we're gettin' close."

He undid his seatbelt and reached into the backseat. He swung the AR-15 into the front, barely missing the side of my head.

I pushed the barrel down to the floorboard. "Are you nuts?"

Mick gave me a surprised look. "That freaky Romeo, or whatever the hell his name is, is one big motherfucker. I ain't taken no chances."

CHAPTER 37

Saturday afternoon

It was Karolek and Romeo. When we were within a hundred yards of them, I slowed down and honked the horn. Both were now inside the Mercedes, which was on its side and covered with mud and vegetation.

Mick was leaning out the window with the rifle in his arms. I grabbed his belt and jerked him back inside.

"Mick! What in the hell are you doing? You'll get us all killed."

"I want those Russian weenies to know it's me their dealing with. Set those fuckers straight from the get-go."

"Christ! Just cool it."

Cliffy pulled the Land Rover up to the right of the Tacoma. We sat there for a few seconds watching the Russians who had now climbed out of the Mercedes and were watching us.

I let the Tacoma roll forward toward the pond.

I was pretty sure I could handle Mick if he got rambunctious again. Cliffy and his teenage offsider weren't going to be a problem, but I still didn't know who he had in the backseat. We all stepped from our vehicles with the exception of Cliffy's backseat rider.

Karolek and Romeo were covered with pond slime. They did not look pleased with our arrival.

Karolek put his hands on his hips and glared at Mick. "My day not turned to shit enough? Now you show up. Don't tell me this coincidence." He snapped at me, "Why this limp dick old man carrying that big gun."

"Mick, give me the rifle." I reached out. "The gun, Mick."

He made a noise like a three-year-old that just had his M&Ms taken away, but he handed me the rifle. I put it on the front seat of the Tacoma.

"You happy now?" I stepped toward the Russians.

"Me happy? Fuck no." Karolek waved an arm in the general direction of the Mercedes and the pond. "Look at this. Look at this shit."

Romeo crossed his massive arms and grunted.

We all walked to the dripping Mercedes.

"This bad enough, but not worst part. Tusya missing." I thought a flash of real grief crossed Karolek's face. "He take Mercedes last night. Said he was going to find one of our girls. She not show up for her shift."

"You lost another girl?"

"Yeah, Mr. Private Eye. Now she and Tusya both missing. When I pull this out..." He pointed at the Mercedes. "I figure they both inside. Probably dead. But car is empty. You look."

"I believe you."

Cliffy joined the conversation. "How did you find the SUV?" Cliffy's apprentice looked at Cliffy as if he'd uttered the most intelligent thing ever spoken.

Karolek growled at Cliffy. "What? You fresh off boat? Use Verizon GPS tracking. Service usually suck, but tracking damn good." He shook his head and looked at Romeo. "Romeo good businessman. Understand logistics and fleet management. His idea to bring truck with a winch. For sometimes big dummy, he pretty smart. Da?"

Romeo nodded in agreement.

I asked Karolek, "So, what do you think happened?"

"Who the fuck know? What was Tusya doing out in this godforsaken neck of woods? Looking for girl?"

Romeo glared at me as if expecting an answer.

From behind us, Mick mumbled, "I know."

We all turned to Mick, who was looking back up the dirt trail we had driven down and pointing to the low hills behind us.

He said to no one in particular, "It's them damn brothers again, 'cept they're dead. It's their kids. Dollars to donuts. It's the goddamn kids and they're close by."

CHAPTER 38

Saturday early evening

It took an hour to get the Mercedes up on the bed of the truck. We had to switch the winch around, tilt the metal ramp on the back of the truck, and winch the Mercedes upright. Romeo, surprisingly, was a pretty fair mechanic. Everyone participated, except for Cliffy's mysterious backseat rider.

Karolek gave the come-along a final crank. The chains holding the SUV on the truck bed were tight. He wiped his hands on a rag and then tossed it into the cab. "Okay, old man. You know where these people are that maybe have Tusya?"

Mick pointed at the county road. "They're right down that road. Not far. I remember busting those two brothers just like it was yesterday."

We piled into our respective vehicles and headed east down the road. Every few minutes Mick would mutter a "Goddamn, I could of swore this was the road."

Twenty minutes and several wrong turns after we'd restarted our search, Mick pointed out the passenger window and told me, "Pull over."

I steered the Tacoma off the road next to a small grove of trees. Mick got out and began fumbling with his zipper.

Karolek swung his truck around Cliffy's Range Rover and stopped next to me. "This old man full of shit. We never find Tusya driving in circles. I take Romeo and me back to town. You can stay out here all night for all I care."

At this point it was hard to argue with his logic. I shrugged my shoulders and yelled out the window at Mick, "Get a move on, Mick. We're all going back to town."

Mick started to zip up his pants then stopped and raised an arm. With his finger pointing through the grove of trees, he danced a little jig. "That's it! That's the house. I'll be goddamned." He turned around and jogged back to the Tacoma, tugging up his zipper.

Through the trees, we could barely make out a weathered wooden structure. It was about a quarter mile away, across an overgrown field.

Mick climbed in. "Head up the road a hundred yards. There should be a drive that goes back to the house."

I spoke out the window to Karolek, "What'd you say? Want to check it out?"

Karolek gave me a frustrated look. "What the hell. We're here." He looked up through the windshield at the sky. "Getting dark soon. Make this quick." He put the truck in gear and drove up the road.

Sure enough, just up the road was an overgrown driveway. It was really two ruts with weeds a foot high growing up the middle. A lot of the weeds had been crushed over. There were fresh tire tracks in the mud. Someone had driven down it recently.

Karolek parked the truck on the side of the road. We wedged in behind him.

Romeo got out of the passenger's side armed with an assault rifle. Karolek got out on his side with a large revolver in one hand and what looked like an Uzi in the other. They went to the ruts and waited for us.

I looked at Mick, Cliffy and his protégée, and the two Russians. "Let's not walk up this path just to be shot by some farmer. It's going to look a bit weird, the six of us coming in." I glanced back at the Range Rover and said too Cliffy, "Is your friend coming?"

Cliffy shook his head. "Nah. Not a good idea to bring him along now."

From a distance, the farmhouse appeared to be derelict and probably uninhabited.

Karolek said, "Nobody living there, huh?"

Mick muttered, "Maybe. But I'm thinkin' we found something."

I waved my arms. "Okay, spread out and take it slow. If anyone sees or hears something, we all stop and rethink this."

Karolek and Romeo each gave me a nod, and we fanned out walking slowly toward the farmhouse. The weeds were thick and higher than I'd first assumed. There were thorn bushes hidden in the brush. The thorns relentlessly snagged our clothes.

About halfway to the house Romeo got tangled up good. I moved over his way to help him out. He was pulling branches off his shirt when the tomato hit his chest. It splattered out covering the side of my face. He lowered his head and appeared to be looking at the mess it had made when the second one hit his shoulder spinning him sideways.

Then I heard the gunshots.

I dropped flat on the ground screaming, "Get down!"

I rolled on my side and looked up at Romeo. He was still standing with a confused expression and staring at the darkening sky. He raised a hand to his chest and the third bullet hit him in the back of the head. Something hot and wet sprayed across my eyes. Romeo dropped into the weeds.

CHAPTER 39

Saturday night

A bullet burrowed into the dirt a foot from my head. I rolled to my right, eager to find something solid to get behind. A blast of automatic fire ripped through the rapidly approaching dusk.

Next came the sound of Karolek jamming in a fresh clip, followed by, "Motherfucker!"

A few yards away Mick sheltered behind a rusted-out hunk of farm equipment. He was taking aim at the house.

Cliffy and his teenage protégée were hunkered down in a ditch off to my right. Cliffy was on his back gripping a pistol. The teenager was on his knees with his head up looking around. A gunshot echoed across the field and a round hit the side of the ditch a foot from the kid. In an instant, he was down and burrowed in with Cliffy.

Karolek yelled, "No shooting unless you have target!" He'd found shelter behind a pile of gravel. I was glad some sanity was settling in.

I rolled to a tree stump near Karolek. Flattening my body behind it, I held the .38 out in front of me. At the distance we were from the house, my chance of hitting anything was around zero. All I could see of the house was the roof and part of the top floor. There was one other thing I could see. Romeo's boot and pant leg rested in a clearing off to my right. The rest of his dead body was in the brush.

Behind me a car door slammed shut. I looked back to see a shaved head moving at a quick clip around the cars. At first, I thought Cliffy's mystery passenger was making a run for it, but the head bolted around Karolek's truck and dove into the high weeds. I watched movement in the weeds as the mystery man moved to the left. Whoever this guy was, he knew how to flank out and was heading towards the house.

Every few minutes we received regular reminders from the shooter, or shooters, in the house. They still wanted us dead. We were pretty much pinned down unless we made a retreat, and there was no guarantee we could do that safely.

Darkness was taking over, making it increasingly difficult to see Cliffy, Mick and Karolek. Maybe, when it got completely dark, we could work our way forward, or back to the vehicles. I wanted to know where Cliffy's rider had gone.

A round slammed into the gravel pile and got a stream of swear words out of Karolek.

Then, for a while, it got quiet.

From a second-floor window came a flash of light and a blast. The round didn't hit anywhere near us. Taking a chance, I raised my head to get a view of the house. Flash after flash appeared in the windows and the sound of gunfire rattled across the field, but it seemed to me that the shots were directed inside the house, not out of it.

A high pitch scream filled the night air, but no more gunfire. Thrashing sounds came from the house – like two animals in a fight to the death. A couple of minutes passed, and a light came on in a ground floor room.

The sound of a screen door slamming was followed by, "Cliffy!"

I could barely make out Cliffy getting to his knees. He cupped his hands around his mouth and yelled toward the house, "Lucifer, is that you?"

The voice from the house came back, "Cliffy, come on down. It's okay now."

Karolek stood up, peering over his gravel pile. "What the fuck 'It's okay' mean?"

"Lucifer's telling us it's okay to go to the house." Karolek, Mick, and I followed them through the weeds. The house was surrounded by fifty feet of somewhat mowed grass. I used the flashlight from my cellphone to illuminate the front porch. As we approached it, the figure standing there shielded his eyes with his hand and turned away from the light.

Cliffy's voice came from inside the house. "Oh, fuck."

The teenager stumbled out the front door spewing vomit. He hit the railing hard and retched into what had once been a flower bed.

Cliffy stepped out of the house, one hand holding the screen door open. "Nate, you better take a look at this."

Karolek, Mick, and I walked into a parlor illuminated by a single standing lamp. In front of us stretched a long linoleumed hallway. To the right of the hallway a flight of stairs went up to the second floor. To our left was an open doorway with stairs leading down into a cellar.

The scarred linoleum was blood splattered, as were most of the hallway walls. The soles on a pair of work boots stared at us from the far end of the hall.

Mick walked to the boots. "Jesus H. Christ." He turned back at us. "What a fucking mess."

Attached to the boots and sprawled on the floor was an obese body. Its nearly detached head rested just inside the kitchen. The body was arched at an unnatural angle with the arms pulled around, under its back.

"He fought hard."

I turned, shining the flashlight on the figure standing in the parlor. Was it another of Cliffy's protégées? Hard to tell. I assume it was male and at some time in the past had a face. Maybe he was once handsome, a real charmer. Or maybe he'd been homely and withdrawn. Just couldn't tell. Burns was my first thought. He had no hair or eyebrows. A nose had been reconstructed between two sunken eyes. The mouth was a hole without lips. His facial skin had been replaced by scar tissue and blue veins ran across his cheeks. A hand came up to block the light. It was covered with the same scar tissue. The index finger was missing.

I lowered the light.

Karolek asked, "You're Lucifer?"

"Yeah."

"You do this?"

"Yeah."

"With what?"

Lucifer's other hand came up holding a two-foot piece of thin wire. At each end of the wire were wood handles about six inches long. Blood dripped off the lower handle. I'd seen this type of weapon twice before, once in Iraq and once in Afghanistan. A few U. S. Army *professional*, probably Delta Force types, were said to use garrotes. A slight few of Orlando's pals at Amber Waves were known to be proficient with the weapon. Torres once gave me a quick lesson that left me with no desire to ever use the skill.

Mick discovered his cellphone had a flashlight. He shone it down the basement steps. "This was where I took out one brother." He reached for the handrail and took the first step down.

Cliffy said, "Watch your step, you old fool." Then he followed him down the stairs.

"Watch your mouth, punk." Came the reply.

I reached over to the wall and flipped a light switch at the top of the stairs. The basement lit up.

A few seconds later Mick's voice came up the stairs repeating his initial statement from the hallway. "Jesus H. Christ."

CHAPTER 40

Sunday morning

"And I let my kid hang out with you?" Art's head was in his hands, a familiar position when he was upset. "I must be out of my mind." He looked up. "When Margaret finds out about what you've been up to, she's going to kill us both." The heels of his hands pressed into his eye sockets.

We were at police headquarters – me, Karolek, Mick, Lucifer, Cliffy, and his protégée. The homicide detectives kept us separated. The good news was that we all gave them pretty much the same story. All be it, six different points of view. After four hours of questioning, Art decided we were not blowing smoke up his ass.

Shortly after Mick's discovery of the basement slaughterhouse, I convinced Karolek and Mick we needed to call the police. Karolek used some Russian sleight of hand and got rid of the Uzi. With the possible exception of Lucifer's garrote, the rest of our weapons were legal.

Art sounded really tired. He was still trying to figure out what to do about the garrote. "This guy, Lucifer. You know who he is?"

I shook my head. "No. Some guy Cliffy found."

"A real piece of work." Art studied the printout in his hand. He handed me the sheet, scooted his chair back, and crossed his legs. "He's what our citizenry now like to call an *American*

Hero. A real combat vet. Frankly, I'm surprised Orlando and his pals haven't recruited this guy by now. Our government teaches these kids to kill in ways that are unimaginable to most sane folks. Then they're dumped back into society with those skills and little else." He threw his hands in the air. "Hell, even Donnie came out of Vietnam in better condition."

The door burst open behind me. Margaret's lab coat brushed my arm as she took the seat next to me.

I started to stand up.

"Sit down!" Her eyes were leveled on me. There was a storm building behind those gorgeous brown irises. She placed a laptop on her knees.

"Hi, Margaret," I gave her one of my best smiles.

She glared at me. The lightning flashes were building to a crescendo. Something told me this might be a good time to shut up.

Many tense seconds passed before she even allowed a miniscule breath of air to escape her lips. Did I see a slight relaxation of her neck muscles? Probably not.

Art was a wise man. He didn't say anything, either.

"Nate, you're one lucky guy." The thunderstorm was coming my way.

"I am?"

"Very lucky. My husband..." she impatiently motioned toward Art, "...can cook."

I was now sure it was time to keep quiet.

"Do you know why it's a good thing he can cook? Otherwise, your godson might as well starve."

I nodded my head.

"I'm going to be in the damn lab downstairs 24/7. Until the swallows come back to Capistrano." She took a breath. "That'll be sometime next year."

Margaret opened the laptop. Her fingers were a blur as they flew over the keyboard.

She swung the screen around so both Art and I could see it. An image of a freshly plowed field with pine trees in the background filled the screen.

"This was taken behind the farmhouse. The K9 body retrievers sniffed out a fresh grave there. It had two bodies in it."

Like an idiot, I said, "That's a stroke of luck."

"Luck had nothing to do with it." She scrolled the next photo up on the screen.

Ric stared up at me from his grave. The head had been bludgeoned, but it was Ric all right. I guess out of respect for the dead, I should be calling him Tusya. Cuddled up next to him was the nude body of a female. Most of her face was missing.

"That is the tip of the iceberg." Margaret scrolled up another photo. "Here's the rest of the field."

My stomach did a little lurch. I heard Art catch his breath.

"The dogs were in a frenzy after finding the fresh grave. Not normal. Our guys kept digging. So far, fourteen bodies. I think it's safe to say we're only starting."

I shook my head. "Jesus."

Margaret closed the laptop. "Not even Jesus is going to help us now. I wonder where the hell he was when all of this was going on?" She looked at Art. "Just before I walked in here, I was on the phone with the team working the basement of the house. They've found over one hundred possible blood samples. The ones we've checked so far are all different. All the surgical saws and blades the team found in the drawers on the tables? I'd say it is pretty obvious what they were used for." Margaret stood up. "Thought you two should know."

She turned to Art. For a moment she was only a mother. "Patty is watching Spidey. You need to get home. He has dance camp at Body Vox this morning."

Margaret gave me one last glare. I didn't catch an ounce of compassion in it. Then, mumbling something about me and my human trafficking buddies, she stormed out the door.

CHAPTER 41

Sunday evening

The sun was setting behind the Coastal Range as I took the first sip of the Occidental Altbier I'd found the in the small wine cooler on the rear deck of Abby's house. The house had two other decks, but this one had the best view.

She was in the kitchen going through the refrigerator trying to scare up dinner. She told me to relax.

I heard footsteps coming up the stone stairs. Donnie stepped onto the mahogany planks of the deck.

He leaned against the railing, glanced in the wine cooler, looked out over the view, and shrugged his shoulders. Then he turned to me and got down to the nitty-gritty. "Have you told her about last night?"

"The essentials."

"Which means what? Jack shit?" Donnie didn't look good. It's hard to put your best face forward when you're dead.

"Yep. That's about it."

Abby came through the patio door with a bowl of guacamole in one hand and a bag of nacho chips in the other. "Nate, did you say something?"

"No. Just talkin' to myself."

Donnie had drifted off somewhere. I don't think he had much interest in meeting Abby. I was positive she'd have no interest in meeting him.

As she poured the chips into a bowl, she looked into the kitchen. "There's a *Breaking News* item coming across the TV." The small flat screen monitor had her complete attention.

We stepped through the patio door and back into the kitchen.

There – laid out in most of its gory detail – was my Saturday night. The body count was going nowhere but up. The police were still withholding the names of the "hunters" who had stumbled onto the farm. The name of the assailant who fired at the hunters was either not known or was being withheld. Apparently, the partial decapitation of said assailant had not been disclosed to the media. But my money was on that tidbit showing up on the ten o'clock edition.

"My God!"

I really didn't have an adequate response for Abby. I turned around and returned to the dip and chips on the deck.

The sun was gone. A bright orange ribbon outlined the old mountains to the west.

My beer appeared to have evaporated. I reached into the cooler for a replacement.

Abby gave me a stern look followed by a grin. "Don't fill up on those. I opened a nice Pinot to go with dinner. How about tuna sandwiches with jalapeno mac and cheese? My fridge is almost bare – and, there's an unopened pint of Tillamook Double Dark Chocolate Gelato in the freezer, if you're still hungry."

"Sounds great to me." I'd welcome anything that would take my mind off the late evening news hour. Which, I was sure, Abby would be anxious to watch in my company.

CHOMPING INTO MY TUNA SANDWICH, I THOUGHT ABOUT

how little of my working life I'd shared with Molly. And, I'd been in love with her. Had been? Still was? Ideally, to *be in love* requires two souls. Molly was definitely no longer one of the *two*. The details I'd shared with Abby so far were next to nothing, and she might soon realize that. I could just imagine opening up to her with the inside scoop on my relationship with Karolek, Cliffy, Mick, and Lucifer. If that didn't send her fleeing off into the night, nothing would.

My relationship with Art and Margaret was teetering dangerously close to the edge, as well. How many times had that happened? Someday it would get a gentle tap and over it would go. There'd be no repairing it next time. Now Spidey was entwined with the three of us. If I lost him…

CHAPTER 42

No time to waste.

Pushing Missy aside, Bernie sprang from the chair, praying he'd make it to the exit door, a good forty feet across the studio floor. He felt every eye in the place follow his stumbling gait. His shinbone connected with a metal drawer protruding from the sports desk. Pain shot up his leg. With his body, he plowed into the release plate. The exit door flew open.

Spinning through the door, he tripped over his own feet. Somehow, and with total lack of grace, he landed seated upright on the second concrete step leading to the ninth floor. He clamped his hands between his knees to stop the trembling. His knees were shaking more than his hands.

Ten feet in front of him, the lime green concrete blocks of the wall started a slow roll to the right. He closed his eyes. Bernie's facial muscles squeezed his eyelids so tight they hurt. Bright bolts of white lightening tore through the dark.

His tie was choking him. He jerked it away from his neck and gasped for air. He held the breath until he thought he'd burst. He exhaled and dropped his head into his hands, jamming his elbows onto the top of his knees.

The door he'd used for his escape sprang open. Missy stood there, aghast, her hand over her mouth.

"Close the fucking door!" He wanted to say, "you stupid bitch," but caught himself just in time.

"Bernie, you look awful! My God, what's wrong?"

The newsfeed, you ignorant cunt. He didn't say that either.

"I..., I..., don't know." He sobbed, tears cascading down his cheeks. Rowdy was dead. Right there on the newsfeed – pictures of the farm, one occupant dead – no name. But he knew who it was. It had to be Rowdy. What the fuck happened? How? The news feed said it was hunters. Hunters?

His head shot up as the door sprung open again. It hit Missy square in the butt, and she stumbled forward. He fell back as her ample breast pressed into his face.

Paula, the News Director, stuck her beak out into the stairwell. "Jesus, Bernie." She spun around and barked at the associate producer standing inches behind her. "Christ on a crutch! Get Charlene queued up!" She turned back to Bernie. Unable to find words, she ran back into the newsroom. The door slammed shut behind her.

Missy attempted to compose herself. She smoothed out her blouse, pulled on her skirt, and sat down on the step next to him. "Oh, Bernie." Missy covered his trembling hands with hers. "Bernie? Bernie, what's the matter?"

His mind was on fire. He thought, "What's the matter? What's the fucking matter? I sure as hell ain't tellin' you!"

She put an arm around him, leaving her free hand resting on his quivering bicep.

At this time, maybe four minutes had passed since he heard Harlan mumbling aloud through the newsfeed script. In a daze, Bernie had walked the twelve feet to Harlan's desk, looked over Harlan's shoulder, and there in black and white was the Breaking News. Headline – shootout at farm – southeast of Sandy – one dead – multiple remains/bodies found on site – hunters stumble on slaughter house – State and Portland Police investigating.

He'd turned and tried to make it back to his desk, but it was so far away. His vision had contracted into two pinholes. His hands gripped the edge of Harlan's desk and he lowered his numb body into an empty chair.

Missy was standing right next to him. He felt her hand rest on his. "Bernie?"

Now, here they sat in the stairwell. On the other side of the door, the whole studio staff no doubt wondering what the hell had happened. Was good old Bernie having some kind of a breakdown? Is it contagious? Is meteorology really that stressful? Is Bernie doing dope?

Bernie stared at the lime green wall. It was slow in coming, but an image formed on the blocks. He wondered if Missy saw it too. As it came into focus, he hoped like hell she couldn't. It was the face of that dipshit private investigator, Harver. Yeah, Harver. Instantly everything became clear – all he needed to do was kill Harver – kill him before the police tied Bernie to the farm. That would make things right. He felt his body begin to relax. By the time the image faded he felt a tropical wave sweep through his entire being. Calm as a day on the beach in Bali.

Missy lean back and gave his arm a soft squeeze. "You feeling better, Bernie?"

They both stood up.

Missy reached for the door handle. "Let me get you some water. You just wait here."

"No." Bernie turned and grabbed the stair railing. He took six steps down the stairs before he looked back up at her. "There's something I have to do and there's no time to waste."

CHAPTER 43

Monday morning

Sunday night, the ten o'clock news had not gone well. The Oregon State Police released more details than I imagined they would – including my name.

Hearing this, Abby scooted away from me to the other edge of the bed. As if for protection, she pulled a pillow to her chest. The light from the TV screen made the horrified expression on her face that much worse. "This isn't what you told me. A strip-club owner and a Russian mobster…, and another dead Russian mobster. And who was the teenager and the other guy, the soldier? Hunters? You weren't out there hunting. What's going on?" She shot out of bed and scrambled to the door. With her back to me, I barely heard her say, "You need to leave."

She didn't have to tell me twice.

The drive home was short – but painful.

Monday's early sunrise hinted at the possibility of a beautiful day, but this is Portland, so who knows? Most of the morning was spent, or wasted, at my dining room table going through mail I'd been ignoring for the past week. I was in the office by eleven o'clock and plopped down in Donnie's comfortable old leather chair with my feet up on his desk. The coffee I'd picked up at Public Domain was within reach as was a peach scone. The coffee was now tepid, if not flat out cold. Sitting there attempting to mentally sort out the overlaps in my personal and professional lives was like doing Chinese arithmetic.

The window behind the desk was open. Happy sounds bubbled up from a one-man band on the corner of Alder and 3rd. He was well into his second rendition of "San Francisco Bay".

Wallace, my hairdresser neighbor from across the hall, gave the partially open door a rhythmic tap and walked in. He immediately headed to my makeshift kitchen. "Think Orlando will mind if I make some tea?"

"Nope. Make enough for me, too." I tossed the nearly empty coffee cup in the wastebasket.

While humming a showtune I couldn't quite place, he reached for the kettle and filled it with water from the sink. "By the way, an old picture of you was on the news last night. You need to get your friends in the media some current snapshots. Profile. That's your best angle. Come over and I'll give you a fresh haircut. You need a stylish update."

"Thanks, Wallace. You're a big help this morning."

"Oh, I've touched a nerve." He plugged in the kettle. "For you, it's hard to imagine the gunfight as being a problem. So, there must be a lady involved. *Cherchez La Femme.*"

"Once again, you've nailed it. Want to join the firm?"

"Not on your life. Look where it got poor Donnie. Bless his..."

The office door burst open.

The peach scone was half way to my mouth when the first shot rang out. Wallace lurched forward ripping the cord to the electric kettle out of the wall. He dropped to the floor as a second bullet hit the fridge next to him.

The barrel of the pistol was coming my way.

My left hand jerked the desk drawer open. My right hand went for Donnie's old Colt .45.

Flame shot from the intruding pistol as I cranked a bullet into the chamber of the Colt.

From my peripheral vision, I caught Wallace coming off his knees and darting to the open window.

My chair flipped out from under me when I dove for the floor.

Another shot rang out and a sliver of wood from the desk buried itself in my eyebrow. Four rounds fired. I was still alive.

Hoping the shooter was still standing there, I reached around the desk and fired two quick shots in the general direction of the door.

Two more rounds hit Donnie's ancient hardwood desk. Thank God, he always bought quality.

I swung the Colt .45 over the top of the desk and let loose three more quick shots. The glass in the door shattered. Heavy footfalls came from the hall. The shooter was running for the exit door and the stairwell.

As I rolled from behind the desk, the stench of cordite filled my nostrils. Bolting to my feet, I fanned the pistol across the room. The exit door slamming shut echoed through the hallway.

Wallace was splayed out on the floor a few feet to my right. There was no blood splatter across the wall or on the fridge.

Two quick steps and I was flat against the wall and peeking out the door. Donnie's Colt swept the hallway. I stepped out behind it. My hands started to shake. Jesus!

I took a chance and dashed to the exit door. My right foot came up and kicked the door open. No bullets pounded into it. Footsteps rattled down the stairs.

I took another chance and hung over the stair railing. A shadow was flying down the stairs five or six flights below. The temptation to fire my remaining rounds was almost overwhelming.

Then my mind jolted back to Wallace spread out on the floor in front of the window.

Shit!

I hit the 911 button on the cellphone.

I ran back through the hallway to the office. Wallace was on hands and knees, and shaking like a leaf. That made two of us.

He rolled over and rested his back against the wall below the window, legs splayed out in front of him. Looking up at me with his fingers poking around his chest, he asked, "Am I shot?"

He looked okay, but I did a quick visual inspection of his shivering frame. "You've got a nice sized welt on your forehead." I eased him away from the wall. No shredded arteries jetted blood at me. "Initially, I'd say you're one lucky guy."

Wallace's eyes rolled back in his head as he passed out.

CHAPTER 44

Monday noon

Art was on the couch usually reserved for my clients. "Shots fired in the Multnomah Building. Now, why on earth would I hear that and immediately think you were involved and know my day was about to turn to shit?" He closed the ever-present note pad and gave me his homicide detective glare. "Wallace might stop shaking by Christmas. I wouldn't want him holding a pair of scissors anywhere near me."

My hands still quivered – probably nothing compared to what Wallace's hands were doing. Gunfights tend to make that happen. I kept them in my lap so Art wouldn't notice.

"The two most recent shootings in our fair city and you're right in the middle of both. Gee whiz, what a strange coincidence." The vein in Art's temple was pounding. I'd seen it pound before – lots of times.

It didn't seem necessary to respond to a rhetorical question, so I sat there like an imbecile.

Enough police were in my office to get a three-on-three basketball tournament going. I'd need to remember to install a hoop over the fridge if these random attempts on my life continued. Maybe, I could cover some of the bullet holes with the backboard.

Sergeant Thurmond put his finger into one of the bullet

holes in Donnie's reliable desk. "Who do you know who's this bad a shot?" He barked a question to one of the uniformed officers over his shoulder. "Higgins, what's the shot count so far?"

"Eleven." Came the answer from the hallway.

Thurmond shook his head. "Christ."

Art's cell rang.

"Mickelson here." He listened for a while. "Just a black hoodie? Running up Alder?" His eyes were fixed on me, but his mind was on the words coming out of his phone.

Art took the phone from his ear, gave it a look like he didn't have a clue what it was, and stood up. "Cameras on the corners picked up a figure exiting the building on 3rd Avenue. Officer Dietz thinks it was a male. Black hoodie and dark slacks moving fast across 3rd and up Alder. We lost visual after that." He put the phone in his pocket. "If this isn't tied to your cluster fuck at the farmhouse, I will be amazed."

I shrugged. "You know what I know."

Art looked at Thurmond, who also had a look of disbelief on his face. "I seriously doubt that."

Thurmond nodded sagely.

I said, "Art, believe me. I don't know who it was."

"I believe you. It's just… with you, there's always another piece to the puzzle. I speak from way too much experience."

When I stood up, I noticed that sometime during the events of the morning, Donnie's leather chair sustained a rip at the edge of the seat. I ran my finger along the vent. "Wallace needs a ride home from the hospital. I need to arrange for somebody to replace the glass in the door, too. Can I go?"

The EMTs had revived Wallace within minutes of arriving at the scene but hauled him off to Legacy Good Samaritan, anyway.

Art waved me out. "Go. Keep your phone handy. We'll have more to talk about before I go home to fix dinner for Spidey." He massaged his eyes. "Margaret is gonna love this."

"She still bunked out at the morgue?"

"Yeah, and for some time to come. Thanks for that, too."

CHAPTER 45

Monday late afternoon

Wallace thumbed a small FOB activating the entry door to his building. Over a dozen of his friends were waiting in the lobby. He was nearly hugged to death before I got him on the elevator. The entourage squeezed in and up we went to the top floor. The elevator door opened and we spilled out into the penthouse condo. Pillows were fluffed, a champagne cork popped, and an impromptu party roared to life. Wallace bravely basked in the TLC. It's not every day you survive a shoot-out. I stuck around for half an hour until his partner arrived.

I'd never been inside Wallace's condo in The Pearl. Nor, had I ever met his partner. It amazes me how you assume to know a person so well and suddenly realize you hardly know them at all. For years, my relationship with Wallace pivoted around the fact we were neighbors on the 16th floor of the Multnomah Building. Most of our conversations and all of the action revolved around the livelihood of Shepard and Harver Investigations. Little, if any drama, was acted out in Wallace's salon. More than a few times Wallace and our other neighbor, a financial planner named Desmond, had bailed me out when things got messy or out of hand regarding one of our customers.

These deep thoughts were ricocheting around my brain when I felt a hand on my shoulder.

"You must be Nate."

The man was tall and trim in a dark blue pinstripe suit that hadn't come off the rack at Nordstrom. His well-tanned face and chiseled features were topped by a mane of silver hair that was almost – but not quite – too long. When we shook hands, his grip was strong.

"I'm Jeffery. The Legislature was in session when the call came from Wallace. A State Police officer gave me an escort all the way home. I've never driven that fast in my life."

TV images of Jeffery were coming back to me – a sixtyish legislator dashing through the halls in Salem – besieged by reporters.

I tried not to appear awestruck. "You know, Wallace mentions you from time to time. Never put two and two together. Nice to finally meet you."

"Well, you can't imagine the number of times we entertained dinner guest with Wallace's swashbuckling tales of Donnie, Orlando, and Nate."

Jeffery was making me smile. It was becoming easy to see how he could charm the opposition at the State Capitol. I said, "I'm sure he exaggerated the events."

"Based on what I've read in the Oregonian, that is highly unlikely." He gave my hand another squeeze with both of his. "Now, I must get to Wallace before all of these queens hug him to death." Jeff started working his way through Wallace's fan club.

I left my empty bottle of pFriem lager on the kitchen counter and inched my way to the door. Wallace was now in good hands – at least until the next time someone walks in my office and opens fire.

As I stood in the hallway waiting for the elevator, my cellphone rang.

When I answered it, a panicked female voice on the other end screamed, "He's here! He's at his mom's! Where's the police?"

CHAPTER 46

Monday early evening

An ambulance with lights ablaze, siren blaring and speeding towards Portland, passed me a mile from Forest Grove.

When I pulled up to the trailer park, the police had the grounds surrounded. No one was getting near the scene and that was supposed to include me. I raised a ribbon of yellow police tape and walked down the gravel drive just like I belonged there.

I stopped a Forest Grove policeman. "Where can I find Gale? The girl who called this in."

His hand went to the pistol on his hip. "Who are you? You're not allowed inside the tape." He pointed back the way I'd come in. "Get back."

"She called me, and I told her to call the police. I called it in, too. My name is Harver."

"I don't know anything about that. I told you to get back." He looked nervous. "Check over by the gas station." He pointed down the street. "Now, get out of here."

"Thanks." I took off at a jog.

Two blocks down, I found an ARCO station. An unmarked Ford sedan idled behind a large blue steel dumpster.

When I approached the vehicle, a beefy guy with a gut struggled out from behind the wheel. His suit coat looked several sizes too small, and his tie appeared to be in the process of choking him. His sausage size fingers clutched a large revolver. "That's just about close enough, mister."

I stopped with my hands in the air. "Is Gale in the car?"

"You just turn around and get…"

"Nate!" Gale motioned to me through the side window of the sedan.

The man turned and looked at Gale, then back to me. "You the guy she called?"

"Yeah." I took a chance and stepped forward.

The cop slid the pistol into the holster on his hip and motioned me forward to the sedan. "We got her out before the shit hit the fan. Finnegan's still holed up in there." He gestured back up the street towards the trailer park. "Put two bullets in one of our rookies. Hit his vest and grazed his arm."

"The ambulance passed me on the way here."

Gale lowered her window and spoke to me. "It's him, Nate."

I asked the big cop, "You guys sure it's Finnegan?"

"We're pretty sure. It's his mother's trailer and the girl ID'd him. A few minutes ago, he started spewing Bible verses out the window. Threatened to shoot his mother and himself." The cop rubbed his red forehead. "A real nutcase."

A salvo of shots rang out. I hit the ground.

The cop landed right next to me. "Fuck me!" He reached over and tapped my arm. "Behind the dumpster. Now!"

There was another Forest Grove officer in the sedan with Gale. The scanner radio was turned up. "Shots coming from the trailer. All officers, hold your fire! Hold your fire!"

I carefully peered out around the dumpster. Up the street more squad cars were pulling up and more uniforms were running into the trailer park.

The big cop's name turned out to be Floyd Mayweather. But he wasn't black and he wasn't a boxer, although I wouldn't want to take a punch from him. We traded a few war stories while crouched between the dumpster and the sedan. Turned out, he knew Donnie from way back when. I was glad he came from the half of the police community who harbored fond memories of Donnie – not the other half.

We sat on the asphalt parking lot for another hour. Floyd decided to go into the ARCO station and find something to eat. He made it to the gas pumps when a single shot rang out. He crouched down behind the closest pump. It was deathly quiet.

The wind picked up and a little dust devil skipped across the parking lot between the sedan and the gas pumps. I realized it was the first dust devil I'd seen in Oregon. A blue jay flew down and started pecking at something in the grass to the left of where I sat.

Then all hell broke loose.

CHAPTER 47

Monday night

"You're sure you have a place to sleep tonight? You won't be allowed back in your trailer for a day or two." I was leaning against my pickup watching Gale fidget in the streetlights.

She took another gnaw at a fingernail. "Mom and I can stay with Jackie. I already talked to her."

"Jackie. She close by? I can put you and your mom in a motel room for a couple of nights."

She gave me a suspicious look and then realized that was a stupid thing to do. She watched the toe of her sneaker move some gravel around. "Sorry, Nate. Guys are always tryin' to get me in a motel room."

"Gale, you need to find a different line of work."

"Yeah? Like what?"

She had a point.

I shrugged. "Get your mom, and I'll take you to Jackie's."

"Last time I saw her, she was in one of the cop cars gettin' questioned, or something."

I looked around. There were over a dozen law enforcement vehicles in the immediate area. "Okay. Let's look for her."

As it turned out, Gale's mom was being questioned

by a young Forest Grove police officer. He and Gale had gone to junior high together, and he was more than happy to drive the two of them to Jackie's. That was fine with me.

Gale started flirting with him before I had a chance to say good night. He was blushing and giggling. Shaking my head, I turned and started back to the trailer park.

The trailer park was locked down. Crime scene tape was stretched far and wide. Stadium-type lighting had been brought in, and a forensics team was hard at it.

From where I stood, the blood-splattered front door of Ms. Finnegan's trailer was clearly visible. I had no desire to view the inside. Floyd told me her son fired a single bullet into the side of her head. An open bible was found in her lap.

Based on testimony from the police officers closest to the trailer, her son began screaming the Lord's Prayer, kicked the door open, jumped out with a fully automatic assault rifle in each hand, and fired blindly into the night.

Jerry Finnegan was dead before his combat boots hit the tiny lawn in front of his mother's trailer. From where I was crouched down behind Floyd's sedan, it sounded like every firearm in the Forest Grove Police Department went off. That may have actually been the case. Later, I walked past two men in forensics' attire arguing over the bullet count in Finnegan's body. One swore he counted fifty-two, and the other was adamant it was fifty-six. I'm pretty sure one round would have adequately done the job.

The thought crossed my mind to call Cliffy and tell him Felicienne's murderer had been brought to justice, but then I thought better of it. This was going to require a face-to-face, and I'd no idea what chain reaction would go off in Cliffy's head. And, Finnegan hadn't exactly been *brought to justice*. He'd been shot to death.

Instead of thumbing Cliffy's number into my cellphone, I called Art.

His phone rang four times. He answered with, "Guess you got the news. There's a real mess in Forest Grove."

"I'm there."

The line was silent for a moment. "Yeah. Why doesn't that surprise me?"

"Gale, the girl from Cliffy's club, called me. She'd seen Jerry Finnegan in his mother's trailer. Told her to call 911. I did the same. I got there in plenty of time to listen to the massacre."

"From the information that was sent to us, I'd say that's a pretty valid description of events."

"You know a guy on the Forest Grove force named Mayweather?"

"Floyd? Yeah. Good man."

"I spent a few hours with him. Crouched down behind his unmarked car."

I heard Art say something to Spidey. Then he was back on the line. "You coming back tonight?"

I said, "First, I need to grab something to eat. Is Spidey still up?"

"He fights sleep when his mom's not here. I think he worries."

"Are they still digging up bodies at the farm?"

Art sighed, "Yeah. With no end in sight. Some of the remains go back over thirty years. God help us."

"I'm not on speaking terms with God tonight."

"That can happen to a guy if you hang around this line of work too long."

"Kiss Spidey for me." I hung up and went looking for the Chinese restaurant where Gale and I'd eaten not so long ago.

CHAPTER 48

Monday night

Cliffy's condo was still presentable. I did notice a pair of underpants tossed behind a potted fern. However, considering it was Cliffy's place of residence, it looked pretty good.

He'd been through a lot of trauma lately. My relating the news of Jerry Finnegan's death barely got a nod out of him. He gazed at the can of Pibb Xtra Cherry-Vanilla in his hand, raised it to his chapped lips, and took a swig. He was somewhere between sitting and lying on the leather couch.

I asked him, "You wanna talk?"

He looked at me and then back at the can. "I don't think so."

I couldn't just leave him there and go about my business. I was beginning to wonder what my business was anyway. "Do you want me to drive you out to the Sweet Mackerel?"

"The contractor had to tear out most of the new foundation. We're way behind schedule. Art just let him go back to work this morning."

He stood up and walked to the kitchen. "Want a Coke?" He tossed the now empty Pibb can in a paper bag next to the dishwasher.

"No, thanks."

He opened the refrigerator and took out another can of soda.

"Cliffy, that's a lot of sugar."

"Oh, you're my mother? I thought she passed away years ago."

It struck me I had never thought about Cliffy's mother – or if Cliffy ever had a mother. I said, "Maybe you should see somebody. Get some help. You've been through too much, and…"

He started laughing. "See a shrink? Can you imagine that. What if word got out?" Now, he was near hysterics. He dropped down on the coach. Tears poured from his eyes. "How did this all happen?" He let his head rest back on the couch. "Everything was going so good. I was in love." That brought on another onslaught of tears and laughter. "You and Donnie. I was always a joke to you guys. 'There's Cliffy. I wonder what the scumbag is up to now. Let's go knock him around some.'" He looked me right in the eyes. "That's what this whole town thought of me." His eyes were full of pain. "Everybody but Felicienne. She saw something everybody missed."

"Cliffy…"

"Save it, Nate. I know what I am. But I know what I could have been, with her."

I walked over and sat down next to him.

The tears continued to roll, but he was breathing normally. He reached over and took my hand.

We sat there for a long time.

Never thought that would happen.

CHAPTER 49

Got to finish this thing.

God, he was jacked!
Bernie stuck his little finger into the packet of cocaine. And... after he'd told Rowdy a hundred times not to mix drugs and booze.

Fuck it. He jabbed the finger up his nostril.

Wow!

The same hand reached out and swept up the bottle of Jack Daniels. It burned all the way down. He took the corner of the bed sheet and wiped it across his mouth.

Damn, this was good.

The sound was muted on the cheap TV in his motel room. On the screen was good-old Missy with a concerned expression plastered across her broad face. Well, it was the lead story, and, after all, it was in her contract to look concerned on a lead story.

He laughed out loud and took another gulp of Jack. She was paid to look anxious or worried – just like she was paid to giggle over the feel-good piece at the end. Usually they finished with a clip of a four-year-old with a puppy, or some such shit, rolling across the prompter.

Well, all of that was behind him now.

A picture of the Multnomah Building filled the screen. He picked up the remote and thumbed the unmute button.

Standing out on the sidewalk was the police detective from the charity dinner. He was being interviewed by one of the station's flunky field reporters. Bernie was thinking it made sense to go after the detective when he finished the private eye. That kind of logic called for another snort.

Jesus, what a day. He wiped his nose on his sleeve.

The cocaine-Jack Daniels combo was telegraphing his brain that he was safe for the time being. Nobody would look for him in this fleabag.

The drive out the Columbia Gorge and up Highway 97 to Wapato was barely a memory and finding the motel was a stroke of luck. He figured the dump must be here for the goddamn illegals. The white trash guy at the desk hadn't asked him for an ID – only twenty bucks.

Bernie stood up and walked to the window. He pulled back the drape and looked down at a half-dozen men in dirty work clothes standing around a hibachi drinking beer. When one of the men looked up at him, Bernie flipped the drape shut.

The police would have tied him to the farm by now. Both his and Rowdy's names were on the deed. That had been dumb – should have handed the place over to his cousin. The property wasn't worth squat.

He inched the drape open again. His Mercedes was tucked out of sight between the two buildings across from his room. He'd backed it as far as it would go into the high bushes. Nobody could see it – nobody except the Illegals and the clerk. A swarm of scruffy kids were climbing on it now. The men around the hibachi watched them and laughed. The damn car was a liability. He couldn't think of a single reason why he'd bought it in the first place. Even if he made it to Canada, it would only be a matter of time before some cop or a Mounty pulled him over. The thought crossed his mind to trade it for one of the pickups or vans parked around the motel. Yeah. That would give him some breathing room. He'd revisit that option in the morning.

Bernie took Uncle John's pistol out of his waistband. It was really uncomfortable carrying it around like that. He liked the way the grip fit in his hand. He could still feel the sensation from the recoil of each shot he'd fired in the private eye's office. Initially, he thought the first couple of shots hit the little guy standing by the refrigerator. But according to Missy and the teleprompter in front of her, no one had been injured. Harver was a lot quicker than he ever imagined. It seemed as if he'd just pulled the trigger, and the private eye was firing back at him.

Bernie realized another stroke of luck – he hadn't been hit. Until it was too late, the thought of reloading never entered his mind. Then he was retreating fast as hell down the hall to the exit door. Six flights down, taking the stairs three at a time, he heard the door above open. He fully expected a hail of bullets to rain down on him but that hadn't been the case. When he burst out into the lobby, he'd jerked up the hood of the sweatshirt, and ran for the revolving door leading out to 3rd Avenue. Running across town with the pistol jammed down his pants luck was still with him, and he hadn't shot his own dick off.

Now, he was a hunted man. The alleged killer. Alleged – Jesus H. Christ, how many times had he heard that bullshit terminology in the newsroom? He jammed another fingertip of cocaine up his nostril. Another jolt of ecstasy fired through his nervous system. Sweet Mother of God.

When the bottle of Jack was drained of the last drop and no trace of white powder remained, Bernie reloaded Uncle John's revolver and unzipped the leather duffle bag. He placed the revolver on top of the money in the bag, $260,000 in cash. That morning, before he'd gone after the private eye, he cleaned out his bank account and the safe-deposit box shared with Rowdy. The box held more than a few mementos the cousins treasured – the hog's ear and a lock of blond hair from the first homeless girl. The only keepsake he removed from the box was an old photograph of himself, Rowdy, and their dads standing next to a tractor in front of the farmhouse. He was probably about ten, only a few years before he and rowdy had started anything serious. In the photo, his dad held the large knife used to butcher hogs. An axe was slung over his uncle's shoulder. All four looked happy as clams.

He wondered if times were better back then, being a kid. Who the fuck knows? All he now knew was that things were drastically changing for him. The coke and the Jack sent him another message – life had definitely taken a sharp turn and maybe not for the worse.

First thing in the morning he'd follow the plan and get rid of the car, find something else to drive, and return to Portland. He knew where the private eye lived – got to finish this thing.

CHAPTER 50

Tuesday noon

We were seated in the conference room next to Art's office – Ruth Dietz, Sergeant Thurmond, Margaret, Art, and me. A gentleman from one of the local TV stations was there, too. His job title was news director, whatever that meant. He didn't look good at all, and he hadn't even been shot at.

I wasn't one hundred percent sure why Art wanted my attendance at the meeting. But with all the trouble buzzing around me, I figured I better follow his orders.

A photograph of Bernie, the weatherman, was pinned to the cork board on the wall. We each held a smaller photograph of Bernie in front of us, except for the news director. His bald head was covered with sweat and his shirt collar was soaked. It must be embarrassing when you have to tell your viewing audience the guy who's been telling them for years to bundle up or not forget sun block was a serial killer.

Art held up his copy of Bernie's photo. "There's strong evidence this guy was involved. Deeply involved. His DNA and fingerprints are everywhere around the farmhouse, on the bodies and clothing of several of the newer victims, and on various pieces of equipment found in the cellar."

By *equipment*, Art meant the knives, hack saws, axes, and other dismemberment tools discovered in the killing room.

Ruth addressed the table but focused on the man from the TV station. "Our suspect vanished – as has his car, a late model Mercedes. It shouldn't be too difficult to locate a vehicle like that. But so far, it hasn't been sighted. He withdrew a large sum of money from his bank account and may have taken items from a joint safe-deposit box he and his deceased cousin kept at the same bank."

The news director tried to raise a cup of Art's shitty coffee to his lips, but his hand was shaking, and he couldn't line the lip of the cup up with his mouth. He gave up and placed the cup on the table. He said, "We've absolutely no idea where Bernie might be. Yesterday he experienced some sort of seizure at the station, just before the news was to air. We pulled in his back-up at the last second." He took a pressed handkerchief from his suitcoat pocket and mopped his brow. "The last time anyone at the station saw Bernie, he was sitting in the stairwell outside the newsroom." He made a botched attempt at adjusting the knot in his tie. "This hasn't been a good month for the station. Our sports desk anchorman died in a fall and there was an ugly scene at a restaurant off Hawthorne involving the deceased man, Bernie, and our female news-desk anchor."

"Strange how things just seem to get out of control, isn't it?" Art didn't even sound sarcastic. "As far as we can tell, the suspect hasn't boarded a plane, a train, or a bus since the incident in Mr. Harver's office. Right now, we're assuming Mr. Harver's assailant is the man in the photo."

I'd never heard Art refer to me as *Mr.*, and he used the term twice.

"We appreciate the station's cooperation. Any additional information related to the suspect should be directed to officer Dietz." Art gestured to Ruth. "Any further questions or comments?"

The news director shook his head, tried the coffee again, failed again, and set the cup down. "Officers, may I leave now?"

Art stood offering his hand. The guy pushed back his chair and got up. Taking Art's hand, he nodded to the rest of us, then walked to the conference room door where a uniformed officer was waiting to escort him out of the building. My guess was he never wanted to see any of us again.

Ruth stretched and said, "Well, that must have been extremely uncomfortable for him."

Art looked at Margaret. "Have you found the dark at the end of the tunnel?"

Margaret was studying something on her smartphone. "And, dark it is. The team thinks we located the last body this morning." She glanced in my direction. "Unless there's another mass grave somewhere between here and Mount Hood, Nate."

I put my hands in the air. "Hey, I'm just the guy who stumbled on to it."

Margaret raised her eyebrows. "You and those human traffickers you hang out with."

I know when it's time to keep my mouth shut.

Thurmond didn't help any. "Cliffy Hasack and Mick O'Reilly? Nate, this is a new low, even for you."

"Thanks, pal."

Ruth seemed to be the only one with any empathy for me. She looked at me and shook her head. I considered reminding her that she was the one who gave me the lead on Mick and Hefty in the first place – but that didn't feel appropriate.

CHAPTER 51

A few weeks later

The case had come to a standstill. Bernie seemed to have fallen off the face of the earth. His Mercedes was found at a hop farm in the Yakima Valley. An itinerant farm worker was shot in the spine by the Washington State Police when they closed in on the vehicle. The hapless guy told the police an *hombre loco* had given the car to him in trade for his fourteen-year-old Nissan pickup.

There wasn't a clue as to what happened to Bernie. The police were as dumbfounded as the bartenders in the watering holes the TV news team frequented. A young lady named Charlene, who became quite popular for her low-cut sweaters, took over the weather desk at the TV station. Orlando told me he never missed a weather report now that Charlene was on.

Margaret eventually got a day off. Spidey wanted to see the Zoo Lights that evening. Margaret opted out, so Art and I took him. When we returned to their house, Margaret was asleep on the couch, exhausted.

The entire forensic team was whipped. They'd found too many bodies. All of them female, except for Tusya and a young man who was identified by Karelok as an "expensive good singer-dancer and talented transvestite hooker".

As the weeks passed and the magnitude of the killing

became glaringly clear, Portland turned inward. It seemed as if the city was searching for its soul. Every preacher, politician, social aid worker, police officer, and sane citizen asked, "How could this happen?"

The answer was dead simple – it *had* happened – and every preacher, politician, social aid worker, and sane citizen had missed it. No one cared if a stripper went missing. Or, in this case, more than a hundred strippers, runaways, homeless addicts – and God knows who else – disappeared over three decades. Well, some folks had cared – Cliffy and Karelok.

It was another cold and rainy morning when Karelok's email arrived in my inbox. The address didn't look familiar, and I almost trashed it. But I must admit, things had become a bit boring, and I was opening junk mail. So, as I opened Karelok's email that morning my emotions surrounding him were, after all we'd been through, mixed.

"Meet me at Daily Café at 10 AM. Have something for you. K."

I finished my tea, washed out the cup, locked the office door, and took the world's slowest elevator to the lobby. The Weather God knew I was about to leave the building, so the wind roared, and the rain poured. I pulled up the hood on my Columbia rain jacket and stepped into the elements. Luck was with me. A streetcar arrived just as I reached Market Street. I rode it to Northrup and NW12th Avenue, then jogged four blocks in a downpour to the Daily Café.

I scanned the open and well-lit dining space. At a table by the windows, four women in work-out gear were having breakfast. Three older gentlemen sat around another table in the center of the room. A lone member of the WWE, whom I'd never seen before, sat at a back table sipping a glass of water and reading the *Wall Street Journal*. But – no Karelok.

The potential wrestler looked pretty young. But my assumption was, from the size of his shoulders, he could pick up one of the cement trucks that regularly rolled by and toss it to Gresham.

The Barista behind the counter gave me a wave. "Hi, Nate. The usual?"

I glanced over the breakfast menu on the wall. "Not this morning. Give me the Morning Sandwich with bacon and an extra egg. I might need the protein."

"Coffee?"

"Sure." I gave him my credit card, signed the tablet screen, took my coffee cup, and walked to the wrestler.

As I approached, he eyeballed me. Then, pointing to the adjacent table for two, he said, "Have seat over here."

He was blond with a long ponytail and the face of a six-year-old. His hands, still holding the *WSJ*, were huge and covered with scar tissue. He wore an expensive Filson Mackinaw Cruiser jacket. I didn't know they made them that big. I suppose it was his attempt to fit in as a Portland hipster. Good luck with that.

I sat down. Before I knew it, my sandwich arrived. My neighbor, showing no interest in me, remained engrossed in the "Business & Tech" section of the paper. Finishing my coffee, I stood to go refill the cup. Karelok walked in. He was dressed to the nines in a Filsen Canvas Gentlemen's Kit and a red beanie. These two guys had been in The Pearl far too long.

He removed the beanie and said to me, "Glad you able to make it." Then he turned to the guy in the Mackinaw. "Get me coffee. Plenty of cream."

The guy jumped up and ran to the counter.

Karelok shouted after him, "Don't have to run. Just get nice cup of coffee." He looked back to me and shook his head. "Good help hard to find."

I asked, "Romeo's replacement?"

"Him? Yeah." Karelok's eyes misted over for a nanosecond. "This one not as dumb. But not as good either." He shrugged. "Whatcha gonna do?"

I said, "Listen, I assumed our relationship had come to an end, now that we know what happened at the farm."

"Relationships funny things."

I had to agree. "That, they are."

He gave me a big toothy smile. His teeth were surprisingly good for a Russian gangster. "You know Chinese yin and yang?"

"Sure."

He said, "Harver, you and me the same. Opposite, but complementary. Is complementary right word?"

"I think it'll work."

Romeo's replacement returned with Karelok's coffee. He stood at attention while his boss took a sip.

Karelok looked at him. "Is okay, Alexei. Sit down, finish paper."

Alexei plopped down in the chair and went back to the stock market.

Karelok said, "You know business deal we make last fall down by food carts?"

"That was a business deal, in the van with Romeo and Tusya?"

"Sure was. You find who was making girls disappear and Romeo not have to break your bones." The mist in his eyes came back. "I miss those two guys. We go through a lot together. Chechnya, Ukraine, Syria, lots of places. Thought nothing would ever kill us." He took another sip of coffee. "Then we come to Portland, Oregon, US of A."

I didn't think he was looking for me to respond.

He smiled again. "Anyway, here we are. Successful strip club operation going. Lots of other business you have to know nothing about."

"We're in agreement. Let's keep it that way."

"Best for you. Best for me."

He put a hand in his jacket pocket, and it came out holding a thick manila envelope. It was taped shut and wrapped in a dozen heavy rubber bands. He put it on the table and pushed it toward me. "This is because Romeo not have to break your bones."

I just sat there looking at it.

"Go ahead. Take. It is yours. You do job. Not your fault Romeo and Tusya get killed. Their own damn fault. Bless their souls."

I picked it up and looked at him. "What's in here?

"Fifty thousand dollars."

"No."

"You earn it. Tax free."

He stood, took a final sip of coffee, and turned to Alexie. "Get car."

Alexie folded up the paper and took off like a rabbit.

I stood when Karolek held out his hand. We shook. His hand was firm and warm.

He said, "So long, Mr. Private Eye."

CHAPTER 52

A week later

The next Saturday was cold, but sunny. Charlene promised the viewing audience a high-pressure weather system was moving up the Oregon coast, and we were in for great weather as far as the eye could see.

I grabbed Karelok's envelope, fired up my dependable Toyota Tacoma, and drove over to Art and Margaret's. Spidey was ready and waiting.

Margaret opened the door. "He's been up since four. Woke me and wanted to know why you weren't here yet."

"He's excited."

"Tell me about it."

I said, "Not every day he gets to go with Uncle Nate and pick out a new car."

"Would you like breakfast?"

"Thanks. I stopped at Blue Star donuts. There's a box in the pickup."

"He gets one donut." She gave me the evil eye. "Got that mister? One donut."

I saluted. "Yes, sir…er…ma'am."

Art walked in the living room with Spidey on his shoulders.

"Nate! I want a red car!" Spidey swung a light saber above Art's crew cut.

He climbed off Art and on to me. Margaret finagled his coat over the light saber and zipped it up.

"Have him home by noon." She pulled Spidey over and gave him a kiss.

Little did I know that fifty thousand dollars wouldn't buy me a new BMW SUV. We left the new car showroom and roamed through the used car lot. It didn't seem to bother the salesman. Used BMWs still cost a bundle.

Spidey was having a ball. He got to crawl around the inside of a dozen X5s. We checked out the engines on most of them. He thought that was extra cool.

"Nate! Over there!" Spidey was pointing the light saber across the lot toward the bay where the cars were washed. "A red one!"

The salesman checked his Apple iPad. "Don't see that one on the inventory." He looked at Spidey. "Want to hang around for a minute, while I check it out.?"

"Yeah!" The light saber cut through the crisp air.

Two hours later I was the proud owner of a Certified Pre-Owned two-year old X5. It was bright red with light brown leather seats and over four-hundred horse power. Spidey was pleased.

The salesman and I pulled both the X5 and the Tacoma over to a far corner of the lot. He promised to have one of the employees from the carwash drive the Tacoma back to my condo later that evening.

Spidey was behind the wheel of the BMW preparing for Daytona while I grabbed my old wool blanket and a box of tools out of the pickup. I put it all in the back of the X5 and then remembered a fold-up umbrella I kept under the front seat of the Tacoma.

"Nate! Let me drive the pickup one more time!" Spidey must of have realized he might have ridden in the Tacoma for the last time.

"Sure. Have at it, partner."

He slid out of the leather seat and tore around the front of the BMW. As I went around the back of the BMW, he scampered into the Tacoma and hit the horn.

A dirty black van almost grazed my arm as it buzzed by me. I jumped aside and looked over to see the driver throw me the finger as he roared out the exit. All that had been visible of the driver was a full beard and two sunken eyes. It sounded like he needed a new muffler as he gunned it up Canyon Road. Assholes are everywhere, even at the local BMW dealership.

I reached around the driver's seat in the Tacoma and felt around under it. Spidey was spinning the steering wheel and making car noises. I couldn't feel the umbrella, so I stuck my upper body around the seat and tried to get a look under it.

I felt Spidey move from the driver's seat to the passenger side and heard the glove box click open.

"Stay out of there, guy. You know you're not supposed to open that." My head was down on the floorboard. No umbrella.

"Nate! Is this your gun?"

My heart stopped. I snapped up and gouged my back on the pickup's door.

He was standing in the seat with my four-barrel Signal 9 Reliant pistol in his hand. He held it like a pro. All he had to do was squeeze the trigger and my world would end.

"Okay, Spidey. I'm gonna reach over and take the gun out of your hand. Okay, buddy?"

He looked at the gray piece of metal and death in his hand. "The safety's on. It won't shoot."

"I know the safety is… How do you know the safety is on?"

He let me take it out of his hand.

Finally, my heart took a feeble beat.

I snapped at him, "Spidey, how did you know the safety was on?"

His eyes were as big as saucers and his mouth dropped open. The tears came in a torrent. "Spidey's sorry… sorry, Nate!"

I shoved the .32 in my pocket and swept him up. His tears were all over the side of my face as I hugged him. "It's okay. It's okay. I was scared. I didn't mean to bark at you." I hugged him harder.

After a minute his sobs gave way to semi-normal breathing. He lowered his head. "I wouldn't shoot you, Nate." No exclamation point. Just his soft breath on my cheek.

I sat him in the driver's seat of the pickup and wiped his face with my hanky. By the time I had the last tear blotted off, he was smiling. So was I.

"Okay, buddy. Now, you tell me how you knew the safety was on."

"Mommy taught me."

My head was starting to spin. "Margaret taught you about safeties on pistols?"

"No, Nate. My real mom. She's gone now."

The things you never in a million years expect to hear.

"Your real mommy, she taught you about guns?"

"She let me shoot them. Just the little ones. The big ones knock me down."

Brigidia Fernandez. What a piece of work, dead, but still reaching from the grave for me and Spidey.

"Spidey, you gotta promise me. Never again… never open my glove box. Okay?"

The tears started again. "I promise, Nate."

I gave him a pretend punch on his shoulder. "I know. And this conversation we're having? Let's keep it between us. No reason to get Margaret and Art upset."

We went back to the X5. I told him, "Climb in your seat and buckle up." Then I put the pistol away in the glove box of my new red car.

CHAPTER 53

That same morning

As I drove my new car out of the dealer's lot, my conscious was bothering me big time. I decided to drive to my condo before returning Spidey home. I'd take the four-barrel pistol out of the car for good and stash it in a safe place in my bedroom. Is there a safe place when you've got kids around?

Donnie would have been all over me for not carrying a piece in the car. Although Donnie was dead, along with Brigidia, both have a way of returning from the grave.

The break in the weather was a nice distraction. Instead of pulling into the parking garage under my building, I drove around to the front and the guest parking slots. In addition to the stellar weather, my main reason for parking out front was Spidey. I'd no idea what trauma he'd experienced two years ago in that garage. Had he seen Ms. Merriman fire the shots through the side window of the El Camino into Special Agent Carranzo's head? I imagine that will remain a mystery forever. Regardless, I didn't relish taking him through the garage.

I pulled headfirst into the middle guest's slot. The X5 was facing the building and sunlight was beaming straight through the windshield. I raised my hand to block the brightness, but too late. There was a blank spot right in the middle of my line of sight. As I slid from the front seat, I pressed the heel of my hand on my right eye in a fruitless attempt to clear my vision.

The sound of Spidey releasing his seatbelt and climbing out of his child-seat registered in my ears. "Stay in the car, buddy. I'll come around and get you."

I raised the hatch and reached in for the wool blanket. Can't have something that ratty in an *almost* new car. I'd grab a clean one from the condo.

As I leaned into the trunk space, my peripheral vision picked up a vehicle in the slot across the lot and behind me. It was an older model black Ford van. Rusty, with a hub cap missing from the rear wheel. It was the same vehicle that brushed me in the used car lot.

I stepped back and turned to face the van.

A man was standing at the side of the van. He started walking my way. When I looked straight at him, I couldn't make him out. But the part of my vision that wasn't blocked by the sunspot saw the big revolver in his hand.

The blur said, "Here, asshole. Put these on and get in the van."

A pair of handcuffs bounced off my chest. I caught them before they hit the asphalt.

"You and me are taking a trip. And then we're gonna party like it's 1999." The man had a beard. I'd heard that voice before. "Don't fuck around. Put 'em on and get in the van."

The revolver was now pointed at my stomach. I felt an involuntary tightening of the muscles and the phantom pain from Ms. Merriman's bullets.

I said, "No."

"The fuck you mean, no?"

"No."

"How about I put a big old bullet in the kid's head?"

"No." I stepped toward the revolver.

"Listen, butt wipe. I've waited a long damn time for this, and I got a real shindig planned for you and me. But I swear, I'll shoot you right here and now and then put a couple in the kid. How's that sound to you?"

It didn't sound loud at all – not like I remembered the four-barrel sounding.

The man raised his free hand to his chest. Blood ran between his fingers. He had a confused look on his face as he turned to his left.

The sound came again, and a red mist covered the front of his throat.

Now, I recognized him.

Bernie's head swiveled back in my direction, and the pistol he was holding dropped to the ground.

He made an awkward step toward me, and his knees buckled. He pitched forward.

I kicked the revolver away before dropping onto Bernie's back. I pressed my knees into his spine and jerked his arms behind him.

I looked back to where Spidey stood.

He was about ten feet away. The four-barrel pistol dangled from his hand, pointed at the ground.

"Put it down, Spidey."

He bent down and laid the pistol gently on the ground.

Then Spidey stood up and stepped back. "Sorry, Nate. I broke my promise."

CHAPTER 54

Several months later

Both Orlando and I received invitations the same day. The letter carrier slipped them, along with a stack of bills, through the mail slot while I was checking out what was new on Netflix. Orlando busied himself with the latest report on conditions at the vineyard.

The continuance of perfect weather resulted in a harvest that was making investors swoon. Orlando and Torres's most recent visit to the vineyard included a sampling from several barrels. They declared the vintage a winner. Torres ventured so far as to call it the best of the decade. I seriously doubted either of them had a clue what they were talking about.

As I was the least occupied at that moment, I went to the door. Flicking through the bills and flyers, I found something unusual. "Hey, check out these fancy envelopes. Looks like we both got one." I handed one to Orlando along with a stack of mail addressed to him. I took my stuff and the envelopes addressed to Donnie – funny how they keep on coming.

Just as I sat down, the office phone rang.

Orlando took a look at the digital screen on his desk. "It's Art. Must be for you." He pulled a switchblade out of his jacket and opened the fancy envelope.

I picked up the phone. "Hi, Art."

"I'm not going. Can you imagine what Margaret will say if she even gets wind that I got an invitation."

I said, "Hold on, Art. What are you talking about?"

"Didn't your mail come yet?"

I glanced over at Orlando. He was laughing – something you don't see every day. He waved a white card at me.

I held up the fancy envelope, turned it over, and saw the return address. The Sweet Mackerel.

I worked my thumbnail under the flap and tore the envelope open. The embossed card inside requested the honor of my presence at the grand opening of the Sweet Mackerel. Black Tie suggested.

Holy shit.

THE FACT OF ART PHONING ME TO DISCUSS CLIFFY'S invitation could be viewed as a miracle in itself. We were still close. Margaret never banished me from their lives, and I was still taking Spidey to Twist, Blue Star, Play Date PDX, the Zoo, and all manner of fun places Portland has to offer. Somehow it was Spidey who kept us together.

Like Karelok said, "Relationships funny things."

AFTER THE SHOOTING, MARGARET THOUGHT IT WAS A good idea to get Spidey some therapy. What drove Margaret in that direction was Spidey's reaction to the whole thing. His reaction was – no reaction at all.

The therapist tried his best, but he couldn't find a thing wrong. No evidence of trauma in Spidey's behavior. Exactly what behavior he was looking for out of Spidey, I'd no idea.

I harbored suspicion that Brigidia Fernandez's genes were hard at work. Heredity can be interesting.

One big thing helped us all. Bernie didn't die. I thought he was a goner as I pressed my knee in his spine until the paramedics and the Portland PD arrived. Neither bullet proved life threatening. Although, the one in his throat pretty much ended his ability to have a coherent conversation with anyone, let alone give a weather report.

Oregon has a death penalty that's been on again / off again for over a century. At the time Bernie was convicted of the multiple homicides it was on again. Several people in the community were disappointed he couldn't be executed more than once. I assumed Art would be an expert on the subject of state executions. He wasn't. Over a beer in his back yard one cool evening, he told me Bernie could linger on death row for a decade or more. The wheels of justice, I guess.

Art conjured up a handful of miracles, and for the most part, kept Spidey away from newspaper reporters and out of range of the TV news crews.

I didn't get off scot-free. Margaret gave it to me with both barrels, and rightfully so. I went through her imposed period of purgatory and came out a somewhat better man. Orlando told me he saw a change in me, maybe more responsible, he wasn't sure. He wasn't sure it was a good thing, either.

My more responsible persona didn't help one bit in my relationship with Abby. She joined a long line of wise women who want me out of their lives.

CHAPTER 55

Two weeks later on a Friday night

The highly anticipated gala evening of the Sweet Mackerel's grand opening finally rolled around. Art had sent his regrets. He tried to keep Cliffy's invitation a secret, but Margaret got wind of it anyway. He got a refresher course from her on the male syndrome which states – even if you bear no responsibility for an event, you'll still get a ton of grief for it.

I rented a tux. Orlando already had one – custom tailored on Saville Row. He looked good in it. Many a stripper's heart would be set aflutter. I assumed he would be the recipient of a multitude of free lap dances all evening.

My ride that night was the Tacoma. I've never been able to bring myself to drive the BMW that often. Maybe Spidey's therapist should take a gander into my trauma. Orlando went on his own and told me he had to pick someone up on the way.

Driving out Sandy Boulevard, I watched the search lights staged in the parking lot of the Sweet Mackerel sweep the low hanging clouds in the night sky. It was like Hollywood in the 1950s. Traffic bogged down four blocks from the club. Not many cars were actually pulling in to Cliffy's new hot spot, but drivers slowed down to rubberneck the scene.

I swung into the newly asphalted parking lot. A large gold banner with an arrow pointed to VIP parking. The VIP pass came with the invitation. A kid in bright gold pants and a purple valet jacket ran up to the Tacoma. He gave my ride a look of distaste and started to back away. He reconsidered when I waved the parking pass at him. I tossed him the keys when he climbed in. He found first gear after a struggle, and roared off to a far corner parking as far from the Cadillacs, Mercedes, Porsches, and a lone Maserati as he could get. The Tacoma is a pretty hard vehicle to offend, so I figured it would be just fine over by the dumpster.

Two red carpets ran parallel up the stairs to the VIP entrance. A line of scantily clad young ladies waited to escort the tuxedoed guests into the club. As I walked to the steps, I looked in vain for the door with the tattered shower curtain.

A young lady took my arm and motioned to the entrance. As we started our assent of the red carpets, I overheard her make a comment in Russian to one of the other girls. Just to make conversation, I inquired if she wasn't cold standing around outside on a chilly night in next to nothing.

"No, this like nice summer day at Lake Onega."

Those Russian girls are tough cookies.

When we entered Cliffy's new digs, the man himself was there to greet each guest personally. I recognized his pear shape backlit by a huge disco ball rotating from the ceiling.

He gave me a dramatic hug and told me, "Everything's on the house tonight." Then, one more hug with a sob. "I owe you, Nate."

This wasn't the time nor place to once again explain to Cliffy that I'd done next to nothing in locating Felicienne and the man who murdered her.

My escort smoothly extracted me from Cliffy and moved on into the club. A surprisingly tight band was playing 90's pop music on the backstage while six naked dancers were on the long bar giving the poles a good breaking in.

We plied our way through the crowd of mostly men. I caught a glimpse of a few gentlemen here and there who, like Art, should have sent their regrets. The mayor's council and the school board were well represented.

The best seat in the house had my name on it. A bottle of French champagne was chilling in an ice bucket next to the table. My view of the pole dancers was unrestricted.

My escort pulled the chair out and fluffed my napkin open. "Barbarella will be your server, Mr. Harver. I hope you have pleasant evening." She drifted away, I assumed back to the chilly, but warmer than Russian, winter evening.

The joint was filling up rapidly. Karelok had done a bang-up job of marketing the grand opening. He bought loads of advertisements on a local porn site. Speaking of Karelok, where was he? I didn't see a single Russian mobster.

I sat peacefully next to my bucket of champagne and surveyed the room. Across the bar in an intimate U-shape booth, sat a strange duo. Orlando in his immaculate tux was seated next to a figure in a dark hoodie. Orlando's dinner partner appeared to be concentrating on his every word. Every now and then the hoodie would nod in the affirmative. I watched Orlando reach inside his tuxedo jacket and take out a folded sheet of paper and a pen. They conversed a while longer. Then the guy in the hoodie unfolded the sheet of paper, placed it next to a candle at the center of the table, took the pen Orlando handed him, and scribbled something on the sheet. He put the pen down and Orlando shook his hand. In the candlelight, I saw scars on the hand extending from the hoodie. They picked up champagne glasses and clinked them together. The guy sat back and tugged the hoodie off exposing a shaved head. Lucifer. Amber Waves' new employee. I doubted this was any reason for the world to sleep a little sounder.

Someone touched my arm and I swiveled around. There stood Gale in her birthday suit, complimented by the thinnest of G-strings and two properly placed pasties.

"Hi, Nate. I'll be your server and companion for the evening."

"Gale!" For the moment, I was almost speechless.

"May I open the champagne?" She fumbled with the bottle.

"Here. Let me have that before you put someone's eye out." I took the bottle and slowly twisted the cork out, just like Orlando taught me. The bottle gave a hushed sigh and a faint mist swirled from the neck.

She said, "Wow. Where did you learn to do that?"

"Private Eye school."

She gave me a doubtful look. "Really?" Hard to get one past Gale.

I said, "What are you doing here? I thought Barbarella was my server."

"I am Barbarella, tonight."

If I stretched my imagination a bit, I did see a resemblance. But then, I'd never seen Jane Fonda in the buff.

"Gale, I don't know how to say this, but I'm a little uncomfortable seeing you like this. Any chance you could slip a little something on?"

"What? You don't like the way I look? I spent over an hour putting the makeup on."

"No. You look great. I just… Oh, never mind."

She poured a glass of champagne. "Besides, Karolek would be upset if I changed costumes."

"Where is Karolek?" I did another scan of the room.

"Probably keeping a low profile. But you can bet he's watching everything."

"I bet he is."

She said, "That new guy who follows him around?"

"Alexie?"

"He's creepy. Romeo was bad enough, but he could be sweet once in a while. Alexie makes me nervous. He's one of those guys who doesn't like girls. Not queer, just doesn't like girls." She shuddered, which wasn't a very sexy thing to do in her birthday suit.

I wanted to give her a reassuring pat, but I couldn't figure out where to put my hand.

We made small talk. She filled me in on her mom and moving back into the trailer park after the shootout. The young police officer I'd left them with continued checking on them regularly and had taken Gale out to the Chinese restaurant a few times. Gale told me she thought he was going to ask her to go steady.

I asked her, "Gale, does he know where you work?"

"Oh. Yeah. He's cool with that. I told him I only give lap dances and don't go with men to the parking lot for extra cash anymore. He picks me up some nights and gives me a ride home in his cruiser."

"Understanding guy."

"Yeah. I kinda like him."

She picked up the menu for the evening and handed it to me. "I can take your order and give you a lap dance while we wait for it to come."

I said, "Tell you what. I'll order and we can hold off on

the lap dance for a while."

I looked across the bar. The table Orlando and Lucifer had occupied was empty. Orlando's mission for the evening must have been accomplished.

The menu had three choices – fish, steak, and chicken. Not overly creative, but we weren't at Ava Gene's either.

A thought crossed my mind. "Gale. Tell you what I'd like. Get me three orders of the steak with green salads, French fries, and vegetables. Get three orders of the chocolate cake and make it all to go. Throw in a six pack of Diet Coke, too."

I took out my wallet and handed her a hundred-dollar bill. "That's the tip for the lap dance we can have at a date yet to be determined."

She asked, "You sure that's what you want?"

"I'm sure." I took a chance and patted her knee.

She popped up from the chair. I made every effort humanly possible not to watch her bare butt bounce its way to the kitchen.

CHAPTER 56

Later that same night

Gale bounced back with my takeout orders in a large paper sack. As I'm always polite to naked ladies, I shook her hand and thanked her for the wonderful evening.

The kid in the parking lot took my twenty-dollar tip and bounded off in search of the Tacoma. I yelled after him. "It's over by the dumpster."

Traffic was minimal when I pulled out onto Sandy Boulevard and turned toward the city. Things got a little more congested at the turn onto Cesar E. Chavez Boulevard. I lowered the side window and let cool air glide through my hair. It felt good.

At Powell, I turned back east. Powell was crowded, but not jammed. I kept the speedometer at thirty and moved right along.

When I got to the light at SE Foster Road, I took a right and started looking for Karolek's club. About a mile down, and with some difficulty, I spotted the brown concrete block structure. Most of the neon lights in the sign had burned out and it needed a paint job. I slowed down. The door opened and a scruffy looking guy in a parka stumbled out. He was trying to light up a smoke and look for his car, all at the same time. He gave up on multitasking, leaned back against the building, and took a drag on the cigarette.

I rolled on down the street for another four or five blocks. The fence was still hanging open. I pulled the Tacoma over to the curb, reached into the far back, and felt around for a flashlight and my winter jacket.

I tugged the jacket over my tuxedo and grabbed the takeaway from The Sweet Mackerel. Cradling the sack in my arm, I switched on the flashlight.

The empty lot on the other side of the fence was as fraught with danger and debris as it had been the last time I'd ventured across it.

The blue plastic tarp still hung off the side of the corrugated steel building.

I swept the light along the tarp. "Hello. Anybody home?"

Not a sound.

As I moved toward the tarp, I saw the pile of rags resting against the corrugated steel. The rags made a slight movement, and an arm came up as if to shield the pile from my light.

"Caboose? Is that you?"

No response.

I lifted up the corner of the tarp. Gravel stirred behind me.

A voice threatened, "I got a knife! You better get out of here. I'll stick you."

I asked, "Ruth Ann?"

"Who are you?" She moved forward a few feet. I could see the blade in her hand.

I held up the sack. "Brought us some supper. Want to join me?"

"Nate?"

"Remember me?"

"Yeah." The blade disappeared.

I placed the sack down on a wooden wire rope spool and took out the six pack of Diet Coke. "Think Caboose would like a soda?"

She said, "Sure. Me, too."

Caboose's hand came out of the pile and snatched the can from me.

The plastic cutlery Gale put in the sack did an adequate job slicing the steaks, which were pretty good, considering the kitchen. Ruth Ann and Caboose sat against the building. I ate standing up.

"I'll save the cake for later. Don't want to make Caboose sick. He ain't use to this kinda eating." Ruth Ann looked about the same as the last time I'd seen her, maybe a little skinnier. Hard to tell. Caboose was still with us, so I considered that a good thing.

She washed off the plastic knives and forks with water from a quart size plastic bottle and slipped them into her jacket. "What're you doin' out here, Nate?"

I put my hands in the pockets of my jacket. "Got a question for you."

She tilted her head. "What's your question?"

"Can you type?"

The End

ACKNOWLEDGEMENTS

Richard Buck and Tom Drews were readers of early drafts of this book. Their straight-forward criticism and thoughts continue to be invaluable. They provide a sanity check on my stories and how I tell them. Guys, thanks for the endless cups of coffee, lunches, and long walks.

This book would not exist without the writing group who put up with me. They kept me honest and true to the craft. My gratitude goes out to Jeanne Davis, Jonathan Penfold, Karen Wutzke, Neal Vance, and Doug Lavan.

Mary Ann Miller steered me through the editing process. Her sharp eye and crystal-clear direction brought everything together for me. Without her I never could have written the book I wanted to write.

Thanks goes out to Greg Jackson and Andre Dubois III at the Provincetown Fine Arts Work Center. Their guidance, experience, and insights related to the craft, and life in general, inspire me to be a better writer.

My wife Kate remains the driving force behind my work. She cuts through my lame excuses, speaks to me in a language I understand, and lights the path in front of me.

Andrea Johnson, at *Andrea Johnson Photography*, provided the beautiful photographs of the Pacific Northwest for my website. Thanks again, Andrea, you're a good friend and neighbor.

Jennifer Utz created and manages my website. Thank you, Jen.

Thanks also goes to my good friend and fellow writer Alberto Rafols. Our discussions on the craft of writing were key to getting this novel published.

The final Thank You goes to my readers. Your feedback and support keep me going. I hope you enjoy this fourth installment. Nate, Orlando, and Donnie send their thanks, too.

Made in the USA
Monee, IL
07 July 2022